TOVE DITLEVSEN

Youth

Tove Ditlevsen was born in 1917 in a working-class neighborhood in Copenhagen. Her first volume of poetry was published when she was in her early twenties and was followed by many more books, including the three volumes of the Copenhagen Trilogy: *Childhood* (1967), *Youth* (1967), and *Dependency* (1971). She died in 1976.

BY TOVE DITLEVSEN

THE COPENHAGEN TRILOGY

Book 1: Childhood

Book 2: Youth

Book 3: Dependency

Youth

THE COPENHAGEN TRILOGY: BOOK 2

TOVE DITLEVSEN

Translated from the Danish by TIINA NUNNALLY

FSG ORIGINALS | FARRAR, STRAUS AND GIROUX | NEW YORK

FSG Originals
Farrar, Straus and Giroux
120 Broadway, New York 10271

Library of Congress Cataloging-in-Publication Data
Names: Ditlevsen, Tove Irma Margit, 1917–1976, author. | Nunnally, Tiina,
    1952– translator.
Title: Youth / Tove Ditlevsen ; translated from the Danish by Tiina Nunnally.
Other titles: Ungdom. English
Description: First Farrar, Straus and Giroux edition. | New York : Farrar,
    Straus and Giroux, 2021. | Series: The Copenhagen trilogy ; book 2 |
    "Originally published in Danish in 1967 in Denmark as Ungdom"
Identifiers: LCCN 2020035114 | ISBN 9780374539405 (paperback)
Subjects: LCSH: Ditlevsen, Tove Irma Margit, 1917–1976—Childhood and
    youth. | Authors, Danish—20th century—Biography.
Classification: LCC PT8175.D5 Z46 2021c | DDC 839.813/72 [B]—dc23
LC record available at https://lccn.loc.gov/2020035114

Our books may be purchased in bulk for promotional, educational, or
business use. Please contact your local bookseller or the Macmillan Corporate
and Premium Sales Department at 1-800-221-7945, extension 5442, or by e-mail
at MacmillanSpecialMarkets@macmillan.com.

www.fsgbooks.com • www.fsgoriginals.com
Follow us on Twitter, Facebook, and Instagram at @fsgoriginals

10   9   8   7   6   5   4   3   2   1

Youth

I

I was at my first job for only one day. I left home at seven-thirty in order to be there in plenty of time, 'because you should try especially hard in the beginning', said my mother, who had never made it past the beginning at the places where she'd worked in her youth. I was wearing the dress from the day after my confirmation that Aunt Rosalia had made. It was of light blue wool and there were little pleats in the front so that I didn't look quite as flat-chested as usual. I walked down Vesterbrogade in the thin, sharp sunshine, and I thought that everyone looked free and happy. When they'd passed the street door near Pile Allé, which would soon swallow me up, their step became as light as dancers', and happiness resided somewhere on the other side of Valby Bakke. The dark hallway smelled of fear, so I was afraid that Mrs Olfertsen would notice it, as if I'd brought the smell with me. My body and my movements became stiff and awkward as I stood listening to her fluttering voice explaining many things and, in between the explanations, running on like an empty spool that babbled about nothing in an uninterrupted stream – about the weather, about the boy, about how tall I was for my age. She asked whether I had an apron with me, and I took my mother's out of the emptied school bag. There was a hole near the seam because there was something or other wrong with everything that my mother was responsible for, and I was touched by the sight of it. My mother was far away and I wouldn't see her for eight hours. I was among strangers – I was someone whose physical strength they'd bought for a certain number of hours each day for a certain payment. They didn't care about the rest of me. When we went out to the kitchen, Toni, the little boy, came running up in his pajamas. 'Good morning, Mummy,' he said sweetly, leaning against his mother's legs and giving me a hostile look. The woman gently pulled herself free from him and said, 'This is Tove, say hello to the nice lady.' Reluctantly he put out his hand and when I took it, he said threateningly, 'You have to do everything I say or else I'll shoot you.' His mother laughed loudly and showed me a tray with cups and a teapot, and asked me to fix the tea and come into the living room with it. Then she took the boy by the hand and went into the living room her high heels clacking. I boiled the water and poured it into the pot, which had tea leaves in the bottom. I wasn't sure if that was correct because I'd never had or made tea before. I thought to myself that rich people drank tea and poor people drank coffee. I pushed the door handle down with my elbow and stepped into the room, where I stopped, horrified. Mrs Olfertsen was sitting on Uncle William's lap, and on the floor Toni lay playing with a train. The woman jumped up and began pacing back and forth on the floor so that her wide sleeves kept cutting the sunshine up into little fiery flashes. 'Be so good as to knock,' she hissed, 'before you come into a room here. I don't know what you're accustomed to, but that's what we do here, and you'd better get used to it. Go

out again!' She pointed toward the door and, confused, I set
the tray down and went out. For some reason or other it stung
me that she addressed me formally, like a grownup. That had
never happened to me before. When I reached the hallway,
she yelled, 'Now knock!' I did. 'Come in!' I heard, and this
time she and the silent Uncle William were each sitting on
their own chair. I was bright red in the face from humiliation
and I quickly decided that I couldn't stand either of them.
That helped a little. When they had drunk the tea, they both
went into the bedroom and got dressed. Then Uncle William
left, after giving his hand to the mother and the boy. I was
apparently not anyone you said goodbye to. The woman
gave me a long typewritten list of what kind of work I should
do at various times during the day. Then she disappeared into
the bedroom again and returned with a hard, sharp expression on her face. I discovered that she was heavily made up
and radiated an unnatural, lifeless freshness. I thought her
prettier before. She knelt down and kissed the boy who was
still playing, then stood up, nodded slightly toward me, and
vanished. At once the child got up, grabbed hold of my dress,
and stared up at me winsomely. 'Toni wants anchovies,' he
said. Anchovies? I was dumbfounded and completely ignorant of children's eating habits. 'You can't have that. Here it
says . . .' I studied the schedule, 'ten o'clock, rye porridge for
Toni; eleven o'clock, soft-boiled egg and a vitamin pill; one
o'clock . . .' He didn't feel like listening to the rest. 'Hanne
always gave me anchovies,' he said impatiently. 'She ate
everything else herself – you can too.' Hanne was apparently
my predecessor; and besides, I wasn't prepared to force a lot
of things into a child who only wanted anchovies. 'OK, OK,'
I said, in a better mood now that the adults had gone. 'Where
are the anchovies?' He crawled up onto a kitchen chair and

took down a couple of cans, then he found a can opener in a drawer. 'Open it,' he said eagerly, handing it to me. I opened the can and put him up on the kitchen counter as he demanded. Then I let one anchovy after another disappear into his mouth, and when there weren't any more, he asked to go down to the courtyard to play. I helped him get dressed and sent him down the kitchen stairs. From the window I could keep an eye on him playing. Then I was supposed to clean house. One of the items said: 'Carpet sweeper over the rugs.' I took hold of the heavy monstrosity and navigated it onto the big red carpet in the living room. To try it out, I drove it over some threads which, however, did not disappear. Then I shook it a little and fiddled with the mechanism so that the lid opened and a whole pile of dirt fell out onto the carpet. I couldn't put it back together again; since I didn't know what to do with the dirt, I kicked it under the rug, which I stamped on a bit to even out the pile. During these exertions, it had gotten to be ten o'clock and I was hungry. I ate the first of Toni's meals and fortified myself with a couple of vitamins. Then came the next item: 'Brush all of the furniture with water.' I stared astonished at the note and then around at the furniture. It was strange, but that must be what was done here. I found a good stiff brush, poured cold water into a basin and again started in the living room. I scrubbed steadily and conscientiously until I'd done half of the grand piano. Then it dawned on me that something was terribly wrong. On the fine, shiny surface, the brush had left hundreds of thin scratches and I didn't know how I was going to remove them before the woman came home. Terror crept like cold snakes over my skin. I took the note and again read: 'Brush *all* of the furniture with water.' Whatever way I interpreted the order, it was clear enough and didn't exempt the

grand piano. Was it possible that it wasn't a piece of furniture?
It was one o'clock and the woman came home at five. I felt
such a burning longing for my mother that I didn't think
there was any time to waste. Quickly I took off my apron,
called Toni from the window, explaining to him that we
were going to look at toy stores. He came upstairs and got
dressed and, with him in hand, I raced through Vesterbrogade so he could hardly keep up. 'We're going home to my
mother,' I said, out of breath, 'to have anchovies.' My mother
was very surprised to see me at that time of day, but when we
came inside and I told her about the scratched grand piano,
she burst out laughing. 'Oh God,' she gasped, 'did you really
brush the piano with water? Oh no, how could anybody be so
dumb!' Suddenly she grew serious. 'Look here,' she said, 'it's
no use you going back there. We can certainly find you
another job.' I was grateful but not especially surprised. She
was like that, and if it had been up to her, Edvin could have
changed apprenticeships. 'Yes,' I said, 'but what about Father?'
'Oh,' she said, 'we'll just tell him the story about Uncle
William – Father can't stand that kind of thing.' A light-
hearted mood possessed us both, like in the old days, and
when Toni cried for anchovies, we took him with us down to
Istedgade and bought two cans for him. A little before four
o'clock, my mother and the boy went back to Mrs Olfertsen's,
where my mother got back the apron and the school bag. I
never found out what was said about the damaged grand
piano.

2

I'm working in a boarding house on Vesterbrogade near Fri-hedsstøtten. It would be just as unthinkable for my mother to send me to another part of the city as to America. I start at eight o'clock every morning and work twelve hours in a sooty, greasy kitchen where there's never any peace or rest. When I get home in the evening, I'm much too tired to do anything except go to bed. 'This time,' says my father, 'you have to stay at your job.' My mother also thinks that it's good for me to be working, and besides, the trick with Uncle William can't be repeated. The only thing I think about is how I can get out of this dreary existence. I don't write poetry anymore since noth-ing in my daily life inspires me to do so. I don't go to the library either. I'm off every Wednesday afternoon after two o'clock, but then I go straight home to bed too. The boarding house is owned by Mrs Petersen and Miss Petersen. They are mother and daughter, but I think they look like they're about the same age. Besides me there's a sixteen-year-old girl whose name is Yrsa. She's way above me, because when the boarders eat, she puts on a black dress, a white apron, and a white cap and bus-tles back and forth with the heavy platters. She's the serving girl and waits on the guests. In two years, the ladies promise me, I'll also be allowed to serve and get forty kroner a month like Yrsa. Now I get thirty. It's my job to see that there's always a fire in the stove, to clean the rooms of the three lodgers, the bathroom, and the kitchen. Even though I rush through everything, I'm always behind with it all. Miss Petersen scolds, 'Didn't your mother ever teach you to wring out a rag? Haven't you ever cleaned a bathroom before? Why are you making faces? For your sake I hope you never encounter anything more difficult than this!' Yrsa is little and thin, and she has a narrow, pale face with a snub nose. When the ladies take a nap before dinner, we drink a cup of coffee at the kitchen counter and she says, 'If you didn't always have black fingernails, you'd be allowed to serve. That's what I heard Mrs Petersen say.' Or, 'If you washed your hair once in a while, the guests would be allowed to see you, I'm sure of that.' For Yrsa there's nothing in the world outside of the boarding house and no higher goal than to rush around the table at every mealtime. I don't reply to either her or the ladies' remarks, which come like pellets from a slingshot and never really hit the mark. While Yrsa and I do the dishes and the ladies cook in the big pots on the stove behind us, they talk about their illnesses that drive them from doctor to doctor, because they're not satisfied with any of them. They have gallstones, hardening of the arteries, high blood pressure, aches everywhere, mysterious internal pains, and gloomy warnings from their stomachs every time they've eaten. On Sundays they march past the Home for the Disabled on Grønningen in order to get into a better mood by looking at the invalids; and in general they put everything and everyone down with nasty pleasure. They have something in particular against each boarder and they know everything about their private lives, the intimate details of which they discuss while they dish out the food on to Yrsa's platters, complaining about how much those people can eat. Sometimes I think that their low, mean thoughts penetrate my skin so I can hardly breathe. But most of the time I find this life intolerably boring and recall with sorrow my variable and eventful childhood. In that narrow strip of the day when I'm awake enough to talk with my mother a little, I ask her about what's happening in the building and in the family and greedily devour every refreshing bit of news. Gerda is working at Carlsberg now, and her mother stays home to take care of the baby. Ruth has begun to go around with boys. 'You could have expected that,' says my mother. 'You should never adopt other people's children.' Edvin has lost his job and has started to come by the apartment again. 'But you shouldn't feel bad about it,' says my mother, 'because now he doesn't cough so much.' It still shakes me a little, because my father always said that skilled workers could never be unemployed. 'My God,' says my mother excitedly, 'I almost forgot to tell you that Uncle Carl is in the hospital. He's terribly sick, and it's no wonder, considering how he's lived. Aunt Rosalia is over there every day, but it really will be best for her if he dies. And margarine has gone up two øre in Irma – isn't that steep?' 'So it costs forty-nine øre,' I say because I've always kept up on the prices, since I've either gone shopping with my mother or by myself. 'If only Father can stay at the Ørsted Works,' she says. 'Now he's been there three months – even though it's no fun working at night.' Her chattering voice spins softly around me in the growing darkness until I fall asleep with my arms on the table.

One evening I wake up as usual from this position at the sound of the clinking cups and the smell of coffee. As I sleepily raise my head, my eye is caught by a name in the newspaper: Editor Brochmann. I stare at it wide awake, and slowly I realize that it's an obituary. It hits me like the lash of a whip. It never occurred to me that he could die before the two years were up. I feel like he's deserted me and left me behind in the world without the slightest hope for the future. My mother pours the coffee and puts the pot down over his name. 'Drink now,' she says and settles herself on the other side of the table. She says, 'Pretty Ludvig has been put in an institution. His mother died, you know, and then they just came and took him away.' 'Yes,' I say and again feel that we're infinitely far from each other. She says, 'It'll be nice for you when you can get that bicycle. There's only two months left.' 'Yes,' I say. I pay ten kroner a month at home, ten are put in the bank for my old age, and the remaining ten are my own. At the moment I couldn't care less about that bicycle – about anything. I drink my coffee and my mother says, 'You're so quiet, there's nothing the matter, is there?' She says it sharply, because she only likes me if my soul is resting completely in hers and I don't keep any secret part of it to myself. 'If you don't stop being so strange,' she says, 'you'll never get married.' 'I don't want to anyway,' I say, even though I'm sitting there considering that desperate alternative. I think about my childhood ghost: the stable skilled worker. I don't have anything against a skilled worker; it's the word 'stable' that blocks out all bright future dreams. It's as gray as a rainy sky when no bright ray of sun trickles through. My mother gets up. 'Well,' she says, 'we've got to go to bed. We have to get up early, you know. Good night,' she says from the door, looking suspicious and offended. When she's gone, I move the coffee-pot and read the obituary again. There's a black cross over the name. I see his kind face before me and hear his voice, 'Come back in a couple of years, my dear.' My tears fall on the words and I think this is the hardest day of my life.

3

I sank into a long-lasting stupor that robbed me of all ini-
tiative. 'You're going around asleep,' said the ladies, whose
reproaches made less of an impression on me than ever. I lost
the desire to talk with my mother, and one evening when
Edvin came with an invitation from Thorvald, I said no. I
had no desire to go out dancing with that young man who
had liked my poems. Maybe his father knew another editor
who would also die before I was old enough to write real,
grown-up poems. I'd gotten cold feet and didn't dare expose
myself to any more disappointments. Summer had come.
When I went home in the evening, the fresh breeze cooled
my stove-flushed cheeks like a silk handkerchief, and young
girls in light dresses walked hand in hand with their sweet-
hearts. I felt very alone. Of the girls in the trash-can corner,
Ruth was the only one I knew now, and she always yelled
'Hi' to me when I went through the courtyard. I looked
up at the front building's wall, flooded with life and mem-
ories, my childhood's wailing wall, behind which people ate
and slept and argued and fought. Then I went up the stairs
in my red dress with blue polka dots and puff sleeves – the

only summer dress I had. Sometimes Jytte was sitting in the living room, smoking cigarettes, which she also offered to my mother. My mother smoked awkwardly and ineptly and always got smoke in her eyes. Now Jytte was working in a tobacco factory. My father said that she stole the cigarettes, but my mother didn't care. She always had to have a girl-friend who was much younger than her, because she was so youthful. But there were gray streaks in her black hair and she had put on weight around her hips. That's why she often went to the steambaths at the public bathhouse on Lyrskov-gade, and when she came home, she gleefully told us about how terribly fat all the other women were.

One evening the boarding house's kitchen doorbell rang, and when I opened the door, Ruth was standing outside. 'Hi,' she said, smiling, 'are you going home now? There's some-thing I want to tell you.' 'Yes,' I said, 'just wait outside.' I poured out the last of the dishwater, took off my apron, and slipped out to her, as if she were a secret contact that no one must discover. What did she want with me? It was a long time since anyone had wanted me for anything. She had on a white muslin dress with a wide, black patent leather belt around her waist and short sleeves. She was wearing lipstick and her eyebrows were plucked like my mother's. Even though she was still slightly built, she seemed to me very grown-up in appearance. We didn't speak until we reached the street, but then Ruth began to chatter on as if there'd never been any question of a separation between us. She told me that Minna had finished school and now had a live-in job in Østerbro. 'In Østerbro?' I repeated, dumbfounded. 'Yes,' said Ruth, 'but she's always had a screw loose.' It didn't fill me with the joy you would have expected. I just thought that Ruth never missed anyone. She had written Minna off with a shrug of her shoulders, just as she presumably had written me off a year ago. There was no room for deep or lasting feelings in her heart. When we reached Sundevedsgade, where I usually turned off, we stopped. 'But you know,' said Ruth, 'you haven't even heard what I wanted to tell you.' Reluctantly I continued on with her, because now my mother would have to wait for me in vain, and if too much time passed, she'd go over to the boarding house and ask for me. Then when she found out that I'd left, she would be sure that some accident had occurred. But Ruth radiated faintly some of the old magic and power to get me to do things that I never would think of myself. Ruth said that she had a sweetheart, a boy sixteen years old, whose name was Ejvind and who lived on Amerikavej. He was an apprentice mechanic and someday they would get married. He had taken her virginity, and it was 'damned great'. And then she'd gotten to know a very rich man who was an anti-quarian bookseller and lived on Gammel Kongevej. It was him that she wanted me to visit with her. She had visited him alone but he'd tried to seduce her, and that, she said, she wouldn't do to Ejvind. The rich man was named Mr Krogh, and his best friend was Holger Bjerre, whom he was going to persuade to make Ruth a chorus girl. 'You too,' she said, 'he's promised me.' 'Me?' A gleam of hope streaks through my soul. A chorus girl is onstage dancing every evening, and in the daytime she can do whatever she wants. I know, of course, that they'd never permit it at home, but the world is never totally real when I'm with Ruth. 'And you know what,' she says eagerly, 'he's very old and he's sick, too. When I was over there, I thought he was going to die of a heart attack, he coughed and puffed and gasped so much. He lives all alone and if we're really nice to him, maybe he'll will us every-thing he owns, and then Ejvind can get his own workshop.'

She looks up at me delightedly, with her clear, strong eyes, and the crazy plan puts me in a good mood. I know very well what it is Ruth wants of me, and I say, 'I won't do it, but I'd like to meet him.' Ruth laughs and holds her hand in front of her mouth while wiping her nose with her thumb at the same time. She says that he looks horrid, but I should think about the money and our future as chorus girls. Mr Krogh lives on the top floor of a building that doesn't at all look like it houses millionaires. When we've rung the bell, we hear a violent coughing on the other side of the door. 'There, you can hear he's not long for this world, by God,' whispers Ruth. After a lengthy rattling with security chains and keys, the door is opened a crack and Mr Krogh's face appears. He looks at us suspiciously for a moment, then he loosens the chain and lets us come in. 'Oh,' I exclaim, 'what a lot of books!' The living room is practically wallpapered with books and large paintings like I've otherwise only seen in museums. Mr Krogh doesn't say anything until we sit down. He looks at me intently and asks kindly, 'Do you like books?' 'Yes,' I say and look at him more closely. He's not as old as Ruth said, but not young either. He's completely bald and has plump, red cheeks, as if he were out in the fresh air a lot. His eyes are brown and a little melancholy like my father's. I like him very much and sense that he likes me too. He makes coffee for us and Ruth asks whether he has spoken to Holger Bjerre. 'No . . . I'm afraid he's on vacation right now.' When he looks at Ruth, his glance slides searchingly up and down her body, but luckily he doesn't seem to be interested in mine. He offers us cakes and talks about the fine weather and about the city's young girls who spring up from the cobblestones like flowers. 'It is,' he says, 'a refreshing sight.' Ruth is bored and kicks my legs under the table. I say, 'Do you think I could be a chorus girl too, Mr Krogh?' 'You!' he says astonished. 'No, you're not suited for that at all.' 'Yes, she is,' protests Ruth, 'if she gets a permanent and makeup and things like that. She's pretty without clothes on.' I blush and for the first time in my life I feel irritated with Ruth. Mr Krogh looks from her to me and says, 'How in the world did you two ever find each other?' I ask if I can take a look at his books, and when he hears that I prefer reading poems, he shows me where they are. I take out a volume at random and open it. Delighted and happy, I read:

– the pitchers are filled with wine,
the twilight-veiled earth.

Baudelaire: *Les fleurs du mal* I read on the title page, and I go over to Mr Krogh and ask him how it's pronounced. He tells me and says that I can borrow the book if I promise to return it. I promise and sit down again at the table. Only now do I notice that Mr Krogh is in his dressing gown. He has a coughing fit again, during which he turns bright red in the face and, wheezing for air, he asks Ruth to thump him on the back. While she does this, she laughs soundlessly at me, but I don't laugh back. Between Mr Krogh and me there's a silent understanding that I don't remember having experienced with anyone else before. I wish fiercely that he were my father or my uncle. Ruth notices this and frowns, annoyed. 'I have to go home,' she says sulkily, 'I'm going to meet Ejvind.' When we're about to leave, Mr Krogh tries to kiss Ruth but she turns her sweet face away, and I feel sorry for him. I wouldn't have anything against kissing him but he just gives me his hand and says, 'You can borrow all the books from me that you like, just as long as I get them back. I'm always home this time of the evening.' When I get home, my mother is sitting at the table with a swollen face and red eyes. She asks me where in heaven's name I've been and where I got that book from. I say that I've been over at Edvin's and that his cough really has gotten better. The book I borrowed from one of the lodgers. When I get into bed, the thought strikes me with terror that Mr Krogh could die like my editor. I desire with all my heart to make contact with a world that seems to consist entirely of sick old men who might keel over at any moment, before I myself have grown old enough to be taken seriously.

4

Uncle Carl is dead. 'He died quietly in his sleep,' says Aunt Rosalia, and he died with his hand in hers. She is sitting on the edge of a chair, with her hat on and her sewing over her arm like always, even though she doesn't have anything to go home to now. Her eyes are completely swollen from crying and my mother can't really find any way to comfort her. My mother has always thought it would be best for Aunt Rosalia if Uncle Carl died, but it doesn't look like Aunt Rosalia thinks so. At the funeral we're all present, including Uncle Peter and Aunt Agnete, who didn't want to have anything to do with Uncle Carl when he was alive. My three cousins are there too. They're little and fat and pasty-white in the face, and my mother says gloatingly that they'll never get married, and so what do their parents have to be so stuck-up about? She and my father have always put down Aunt Agnete and Uncle Peter, and yet they still play cards with them a couple of times a week. It irritates me when I get home from work, because then I can't go to bed until they've left. While the minister preaches over Uncle Carl, I don't laugh like at my granny's funeral, but I think about the fact that no one except

Aunt Rosalia has known him or knew what he was really like. First he was a hussar, then he was a blacksmith, then he drank beer, and finally soda pop. That's all that the rest of us know. We have coffee in a restaurant near the cemetery, and there's an oppressive mood because Aunt Rosalia refuses to be cheered up by anything whatsoever. Her tears fall into her coffee cup and she has to keep lifting the black veil of her funeral hat to dry them away. 'He was handsome as a young man,' she says to my mother, 'wasn't he, Alfrida?' 'Yes, he was,' says my mother. 'He was handsome back then.' Aunt Rosalia says, 'I know that none of you liked him because he drank. He suffered a great deal because of that. His own family didn't like him either.' It's embarrassing, and no one answers, because she's right, of course. 'Well,' says Edvin, getting up, 'I have to go now. I have to meet a friend.' After he's gone, I look around at my family, at these faces that have surrounded me my whole childhood, and I find them tired and aged, as if the years that I've used to grow up in have exhausted them completely. Even my cousins, who are not much older than me, look worn-out and used up. My father is very quiet and serious, as always when he's wearing his Sunday suit. It's as if it's lined with dark and depressing thoughts that he puts on along with the suit. He's talking with Uncle Peter in a low voice, mumbling. Even at the funeral they discuss politics, but they don't get excited about it like they usually do. My father is still working at the H. C. Ørsted Works, and my mother has finally gotten the radio that she wanted me to pay for. She has it on all day long and only turns it off when there's someone in the living room she wants to talk to. When my father's home, he's always lying on the sofa, sleeping. Then when my mother turns off the radio, he wakes up with a start and says, 'It's damn near

impossible to sleep with that God-awful noise.' We think
that's really funny. But I'm not really involved with all that
goes on at home anymore – not like before. I'm really only
alive when I'm at Mr Krogh's. I visit him as often as I dare,
without provoking my mother. I say that I'm visiting Yrsa,
but my mother can't understand why we're suddenly friends,
since I've always said that I didn't like her. I borrow books
from Mr Krogh and return them again after I've read them.
He always greets me in his silk dressing gown, with red slip-
pers on his feet; he pours us coffee from a silver coffeepot. If
he doesn't have any pastry, he gives me fifty øre to go down
and buy some. We drink coffee at a low table with an etched
brass surface. Mr Krogh has long, white hands that always
tremble slightly, and he has a low, pleasant voice that I love to
listen to. He does most of the talking when I'm there, because
he doesn't like me to show my curiosity. One evening when
I asked him why he wasn't married, he said, 'You're not supposed to know everything about a person – remember that.
Then it stops being exciting.' I don't know, either, whether
Ruth still comes there, whether she's going to be a chorus
girl, or whether Mr Krogh even knows Holger Bjerre at all.
Ruth doesn't think so. Whenever I meet her in the courtyard
or on the street, she says, 'That Krogh is full of lies, and he's
a dirty old man. Hasn't he made a pass at you yet?' 'No,' I say
and think she's talking about someone completely different
than the Mr Krogh I know. 'Well, I don't dare go there alone,'
she says. Another day she says that he's stingy since he never
gives me any presents. 'Why should he?' I ask. She gives me
a look bursting with impatience. 'Because,' she says, 'he's old
and you're young. He's completely crazy about young girls,
and he has to pay for that – what else?' One evening when Mr
Krogh has lit the candles in a tall silver candleholder that's

standing on the table between us, I gather my courage and say, 'Mr Krogh, when I was little, I wrote poems.' He smiles. 'Yes,' he says, 'and you want to show them to me?' I blush because he's guessed what I want from him, and I ask him how he knows. 'Oh,' he says, 'either that or something else. People always want something from each other, and I've known all along that you wanted to use me for something.' When I make a protesting gesture, he says, 'There's nothing wrong with that – it's completely natural. I want something from you, too.' 'What?' I ask. 'Nothing in particular,' he says, taking his long thin pipe out of his mouth. 'I just collect eccentrics – people who are different, special cases. I'd like to see your poems. Thump me on the back.' The last comes out in gasps, and he gets quite blue in the face. He coughs at each thump I give him and he doubles up so that his arms hang down to the floor. I wonder what kind of illness he suffers from. I don't dare ask whether it's fatal, but already the next evening I rush over to his apartment with my poetry album, half convinced that he's no longer among the living. But he is, and as soon as we're sitting at the coffee table, I hand him the book, very afraid of disappointing him, accustomed as he is to reading the greatest poetry. He puts his pipe down and pages through the book, while I tensely watch his face. 'Yes,' he says, nodding, 'children's poems!' He reads aloud:

> Sleeping girl, I'll sing a hymn for you.
> No sight has ever brought me joy so true
> as you lying motionless and sweet,
> smiling in your dreams, the white sheet
> barely covering your young breast,
> oh, how that sight to me was blest,
> but you were unaware.

There are four or five verses, and he mumbles them all to himself. Then he looks at me kindly and gravely and says, 'That's interesting. Who were you thinking of when you wrote that poem?' 'No one,' I say, 'well, yes, maybe Ruth.' He laughs heartily. 'Life is funny,' he says then. 'You realize it first when you're about to lose it.' 'But Mr Krogh,' I say terrified, 'you're not that old – not any older than my father.' 'Oh no,' he says, 'but even so, I've lived a long time.' He shuts the book and puts it on the table. 'These poems,' he says, 'can't be used for anything, but it looks like you're going to be a poet someday.' A wave of happiness floods through me at these words. I tell him about Editor Brochmann, who said that I should come back in a couple of years, and he says that he knew him well. He also says that someday when I write something good, something that other people will take pleasure in reading, I should show it to him and then he'll see that it's published. The candles flicker in the holder and the dark evening sky is full of stars. I'm terribly fond of Mr Krogh, but I don't dare tell him so. We're silent for a long time. From the bookshelves there issues a pleasant smell of leather, paper, and dust, and Mr Krogh looks at me with a sorrowful glance, as if what he wants to tell me will never be said, exactly like my father has always looked at me. Then he gets up. 'Well,' he says, 'you'd better go. I have some work to do before I go to bed.' Out in the hallway he puts his hand under my chin and says, 'Will you give an old man a kiss on the cheek?' I kiss him carefully, as if my kiss could bring about his feared death. It's a soft, old man's cheek that reminds me of my Granny's.

5

Hitler has come to power in Germany. My father says that
it's the reactionaries who've won and that the Germans don't
deserve any better since they voted for him themselves. Mr
Krogh calls it a catastrophe for the whole world and is gloomy
and depressed as if from some personal sorrow. The ladies at
the boarding house cheer and say that if Stauning were like
Hitler, we wouldn't have unemployment, but he's weak and
corrupt and drunken and everything he does in the govern-
ment is wrong. They listen to the news on the radio instead of
taking a nap before dinner, and they come back with shining
eyes and say that the Reichstag fire was set by the Commu-
nists and now it will certainly be proved at the trial. My father
and Mr Krogh say that the Nazis started it themselves, and
if I have any opinion at all, it's to agree with them. But most of
all, I'm terrified – as if the swells from the great ocean of the
world could capsize my fragile little ship at any moment. I
don't like reading the newspapers anymore, but I can't avoid
them entirely. My father shows me Anton Hansen's dark,
satirical drawings in *Social-Demokraten*, and they increase
my fear. There is an old Jew with a large sign on his back,

surrounded by laughing SS-men. On the sign it says in German: 'I am a Jew, but I don't want to complain about the Nazis.' I have to tell my father what it means. Mr Krogh subscribes to *Politiken*. He shows me a drawing of Van der Lubbe and the caption underneath:

> Tell us what you know
> about Torgler and the fire.
> —
> You know, we want to know, damn it.
> Say that Dimitroff
> and Popoff were waiting by the stairs,
> then you'll save your neck.

'Oh yes,' he says, 'now the German intelligentsia is in for it.' I ask him what 'German intelligentsia' means and he explains it to me. Among other things, it means the artists. A poet is an artist, and Mr Krogh has said that I'll be a poet someday. The ladies read *Berlingske Tidende,* and there, they say, the truth is written about Hitler, who may save all of Europe and create a kind of paradise for us all. More than ever I want to get away from the boarding house's close, filthy kitchen and the people I'm with there every day. My father is always sleeping when I come home and a couple of hours later he leaves for work. One evening when he wakes up, I ask him whether I can look for another job. I say that I hate washing dishes and cleaning and doing any kind of domestic work at all. I would rather work in an office and learn to type. 'Not yet,' he says, 'first you have to learn to take care of a house properly and cook for your husband when he comes home from work.' 'She'll learn that soon enough,' my mother comes to my aid, 'when she has use for it one day.' She also says, 'You talk like she's going to get married tomorrow. She's only just turned fifteen.' My father presses his lips together and frowns. 'Is it you or me who decides?' he says. Then my mother keeps quiet, but she's insulted too, and the atmosphere in the living room is tense. When my father has left, she puts down her knitting and smiles. 'We'll pretend,' she says, 'that one of the lodgers has made a pass at you. Then you can look for another job.' 'OK,' I say relieved, astonished that I never thought of that before. A couple of days later, my father is sitting on the sofa when I come home. 'Well,' he says, 'Mother told me what happened. Now you've reached the age when you need to watch out for yourself. You're not to go back there. Mother can go and pick up your paycheck, and then you'll have to start looking for another job.' Then I stay home for a while. We buy *Berlingske Tidende* and I send in replies for many office jobs but get no response. I also go around Vesterbro and apply for those jobs where you're supposed to appear in person. I talk to fine gentlemen in big, light offices and they all ask me what my father does. When I tell them, they figure that I'll have to live on my salary and it's never intended for that. But finally I succeed in getting a job where the director just asks me whether I'm a member of the union. When he hears that I'm not, he hires me immediately for forty kroner a month. It's in a nursing supply company on Valdemarsgade and I'm to be stock clerk. 'Scab company,' says my father when he hears the part about the union, but he gives in anyway, because even for a girl it's not easy to find a job.

While all of this was going on, I didn't have a chance to visit Mr Krogh. He had never asked me where I lived and was not inquisitive in general, just as he didn't like others to be, either. One evening I go out to see him again. It's winter and I have on Edvin's made-over coat, which is more warm

25

than beautiful. I'm looking forward to seeing my friend again and to telling him about my new job, which for now I'm happy with. I cut through the usual passageway from Vesterbrogade, and when I reach Gammel Kongevej, I stop as if paralyzed, completely uncomprehending. The yellow building isn't there anymore. Where it had stood, there is just a space with rubble, plaster, and rusty, twisted water pipes. I go over and brace my hand against the low remains of a wall, because I don't think my legs will support me any longer. People go past me with closed faces, wrapped up in their own evening errands. I feel like grabbing one of them by the arm and saying, 'There was a building here yesterday – can you tell me where it is? Where is Mr Krogh?' He must be living somewhere else now, of course, but how do you find someone who has disappeared? I don't understand how he could do this to me. But maybe he knew so many young girls and I was just one of them. He'd said that he collected eccentrics, but maybe I wasn't eccentric enough. As I walk slowly home, still half numbed by this misfortune, I think that this wouldn't have happened if I'd written good poems. I don't think it would have happened, either, if he'd desired my body, as he obviously desired Ruth's, but no one has yet shown any interest whatsoever in me in that way; my father's warning is completely unnecessary. At home on my street, Ruth is standing with her apprentice mechanic in front of the stairwell to the front building. I stop and button my coat at the neck because the wind is icy cold, which I first notice now. 'Mr Krogh's building was torn down,' I say. 'Do you know where he's living?' 'Nope,' she says over the young man's shoulder, 'and I don't give a damn, either.' They disappear into each other's embrace again and I walk past, across the courtyard. As I go up the stairs to the back building, I'm gripped by the fear that I'll never get away from this place where I was born. Suddenly I can't stand it and find every memory of it dark and sad. As long as I live here I'm condemned to loneliness and anonymity. The world doesn't count me as anything and every time I get hold of a corner of it, it slips out of my hands again. People die and buildings are torn down over them. The world is constantly changing – it's only my childhood's world that endures. Up in the living room it looks like it has always looked. My father is sleeping and my mother is sitting at the table knitting. Her gray hair is gone because, in the greatest secrecy, she has it dyed – wherever she gets the money from for that . . . Once in a while my father says, 'It's strange that your hair is still black. Mine is completely gray now.' He's naive and believes everything we say, because he himself never lies. 'Where have you been?' asks my mother, looking at me suspiciously. 'At Yrsa's,' I say, not caring whether she believes me. She says, 'It's cold in here; put some more coals in the stove.' Then she puts the water on for coffee and I decide that, like Edvin, I'm going to move out when I'm eighteen. I won't be allowed to until then. When I live somewhere else – away from Vesterbro – it'll be easier for me to make contact with people like Mr Krogh. While we're drinking coffee, I glance through the newspaper a bit. It says that Van der Lubbe has been executed and that Dimitroff made a complete fool of Göring at the trial. I turn to the obituaries, but don't find Mr Krogh's name among the dead. It strikes me that it was as if he lost interest in me when Hitler came to power; again my little ship trembles with a vague fear of capsizing.

6

I have to be at work at seven o'clock in the morning and, with Mr Jensen, I clean the rooms and put them in order before the office personnel and the director arrive. Mr Jensen is sixteen years old, tall and thin and silly. He blows up condoms and lets them fly around over my head while I'm washing the floor, and he tries to kiss me so that, laughing, I have to defend myself with the rag in one hand. He's just a boy, and I'm not offended by his coarseness. In the director's office, he sits in the chair with his feet up on the desk and a cigarette between his lips. 'Don't I look like him?' he asks, twisting his long bangs around his fingers. He says that I'm prudish because I'm a virgin and because I won't kiss him. 'If you were in love with me,' I say, 'then I would.' He insists that he is, but I don't believe him. One morning when I'm in the process of washing the floor in the director's office, the director suddenly comes through the door, and as I feverishly gather up the scrub brushes and bucket, he takes hold of me from behind and grabs my breasts with both hands. He does it rather like the way my mother touches the meat at the butcher's, and I turn red with shame and outrage and slip past him with the bucket and scrub brushes without saying a word. I tell Mr Jensen about it and he says I should have slapped his fingers because he always goes to bed with the female employees, and I shouldn't put up with that. He's married and has lots of children because he's a Catholic. But afterwards I don't feel very bad about it. He is the first man who has shown interest in my body, and I've gotten it into my head that without that, I will never get ahead in the world. When the two office secretaries and the stock room supervisor arrive, the orders have to be taken care of. It's my job to pack the goods at the long counter in the stock room. Thermometers, absorbent cotton, vaginal syringes, hot-water bottles, condoms, trusses. Mr Jensen has carefully explained what everything is used for, and sex seems to me extremely complicated and not very appealing. One thing is for before and one thing is for afterwards; during Mr Jensen's explanations, which certainly don't present it very simply, I feel quite inadequate. The stock room supervisor is named Mr Ottosen, and the pretty secretaries are openly in love with him. When they stand at the counter with their papers, explaining something to him, he slips his arm around their waists, and they lean toward him, starry-eyed. Two pretty, chic young girls with tiny curls all over their heads, high heels, and wide patent leather belts around their waists. Someday when I work in an office, I want to try to look just like them. I'll try to pay attention to what dresses I wear and how my hair looks. But I put off these exertions because they bore me. I'm wearing a brown smock that the company issued me. When I'm looking for a job, I rub my cheeks with my mother's tissue paper, and that's all I've ever done for my appearance. My hair is long, blond and straight, and I wash it with brown soap whenever I think it needs it. Mr Krogh said that I had beautiful hair, but maybe he couldn't find anything else to praise me for. In any case, I very often stand next to Mr Ottosen, and I've also tried leaning ever so slightly against him, but he never puts his arm around my waist or seems to notice my weak overture at all. I think about that a lot and reach the conclusion that most women exert an irresistible attraction over men – but I don't. It's both sad and strange, but it does protect me from having children too soon, like most of the girls on my street. One day Mr Jensen asks me if I'd like to go to the movies in the evening. I say yes, because ever since I was a child I've wanted to be allowed to see a movie. My parents wouldn't let me. For once I tell the truth at home, and my mother looks very excited. She wants to know everything about Mr Jensen, and in her mind she has me married to him at once. But I don't know what his father does or what plans he himself has for the future, so I can't satisfy her curiosity. My father is very happy that he's a member of Danish Social Democratic Union (DSU) which, to his regret, Edvin won't join. 'Without a doubt,' he says, twisting the ends of his mustache, 'a very sensible young man.' So for the first time I'm sitting in a movie house next to a very scrubbed Mr Jensen, who is wearing his confirmation suit that ends just short of his not completely clean wrists. We've hung our coats over the backs of the seats. First there's someone who plays the piano. Then the lights go out and flashing commercials flicker across the screen. When they're over and the lights go on again, I'm about to get up because I think that's all there is, but Mr Jensen pulls me down in the seat again. 'It's just starting now,' he says patiently. The film is called *The Cabin Boy*, and the boy is the handsome and touching Jackie Coogan. I'm completely enchanted and forget where I am and who I'm with. I cry as if I were being beaten and mechanically accept the handkerchief Mr Jensen puts into my hand. When he puts his hand on my knee, I push it away as if it were a dead object. With the captain, the cabin boy goes down with the ship, sacrificing his life for a beautiful, violently sobbing woman and her little girl. I bawl loudly and can't stop when the lights go on. 'Shh . . . ,' says Mr Jensen embarrassed, taking me by the arm as we go out. 'Why aren't you crying?' I ask. 'Don't you think it was sad?' 'Yes, I do,' says Mr Jensen, 'but to come right out and cry at the movies!' We walk down Søndre Boulevard and Mr Jensen laces his fingers through mine. I give him a sidelong glance and discover that he has long eyelashes. Maybe he really is in love with me. The snow creaks under our feet and the sky is bright with stars. His arm shakes a little, but that could be from the cold. Home in the dark doorway, he embraces me and kisses me. I don't resist, but it doesn't make me feel anything. His lips are cold and hard as leather. 'Why don't we use our first names?' he asks in a hoarse voice. 'OK,' I say, 'what's your name?' His name is Erling, and we agree to still use our last names at work.

Whenever there's nothing to do in the stock room in the afternoon, I'm sent up to the attic to put metal boxes in order in long rows. I like the work because I'm all alone in the dark and dusty room. I lie on the floor and place the boxes in even rows according to what it says on them: zinc salve, lanolin. I sink into a sweet melancholy and rhythmic waves of words stream through me again. I write them down on brown wrapping paper and conclude sorrowfully that the poems are still not good enough. 'Children's poems,' said Mr Krogh. He also said, 'In order to write a good poem, you have to have experienced an awful lot.' I think that I have, but maybe I'll experience even more. Then one day I write something that is different from anything I've written before, only I don't know what the difference is. I write the following:

> There burns a candle in the night,
> it burns for me alone,
> and if I blow at it,
> it flames up,
> and flames for me alone.
> But if you breathe softly
> and if you breathe quietly,
> the candle is suddenly more than bright
> and burns deep in my own breast,
> for you alone.

I think it's a real poem, and the pain at Mr Krogh's disappearance springs up again, because I want so much to show it to him. I want so much to tell him that now I understand what he meant. But for me he's just as dead as the old editor, and I can't find any new wedge into the world that is moved by poems and, I hope, by people who write them. 'You were gone a long time,' says Erling when I come downstairs. He acts the whole time as if we are going steady. He's standing there packing a douche bag (it's used afterwards, he has explained to me), and says, as he bends the red tubes under the monstrosity, 'Why don't we sleep together at a hotel on Saturday? I've saved up for it.' 'No,' I say, because if I can write real poems now, it doesn't matter that I'm a virgin. On the contrary, I may have use for it when I meet the right man. 'God Almighty,' says Erling irritated, 'are you saving it for the coroner?' 'Yes,' I say, laughing so I can hardly stop. I don't really know myself what virginity and poems have to do with each other, so how could I explain the strange connection to Erling?

7

Every Saturday evening, Erling and I go to the movies. He waits for me, leaning against the wall of the front building, his hands buried in the pockets of his father's coat, which he inherited just like I've inherited my brother's. If I keep him waiting too long, he chews on matches and twists his hair in his fingers. As we go out through the doorway, my mother opens the window and yells, 'Goodbye, Tove.' That means she approves of the relationship, and Erling takes it to mean that too. He asks me whether he's going to meet my parents soon. 'No,' I say, 'not yet.' My mother asks whether Erling has a clubfoot or a harelip, since they aren't allowed to meet him. I don't want to visit Erling's parents, either, because then they'll think that we're engaged. It would be both easier and more fun for me if I had a girlfriend, but I don't anymore; so Erling is better than nothing. I like him a lot because he's also a little strange, and he's like me in many ways. His father is a laborer and often unemployed. He has a grown-up sister who is married. He himself wants to be a schoolteacher, but he can't get into the teachers' college until he's eighteen. He's saving money for it. He says that it's outrageous that they use unorganized labor in the company, but if he joins the union, he'll be thrown out. He earns twenty-five kroner a week. I pay for myself when we go to the movies, both because he can't really afford to pay for the two of us, and because I think it makes me more independent. All of these evenings proceed in the same way. When the movie is over, he walks me home, and inside the dark doorway, he embraces and kisses me. I observe him with a certain cold curiosity, wanting to see how excited I can make him. If I were in love with him, I would be passionate too, but I'm not, and he knows it. At a certain moment I loosen his cold hands from around my neck and say, 'No, don't do that.' 'Oh yes,' he whispers breathlessly, 'it doesn't hurt at all.' 'No,' I say, 'but I don't want to.' I feel sorry for him and kiss his leathery lips before I go. He asks me when I will want to, and just for something to say, I promise to do it when I turn eighteen, because that's still such a terribly long way off. I also feel a little sorry for myself because his embraces don't make the slightest chord in me sing. I wonder whether I'm abnormal in that way too. 'Damned great,' Ruth had said, and she was only thirteen. All of the girls in the trash-can corner said the same thing, but maybe they were lying. Maybe it was just something that they said. 'When do we get to meet your sweetheart?' says my mother upstairs in the living room. 'When I met your father, I invited him home right away.' She also says that he's obviously only out after one thing, and if I let him have his way, he won't want anything more to do with me. 'And you can't come back here with a kid,' she says. One evening I say that she wasn't nearly so eager for Edvin to bring his girlfriend home, and she says sharply that it's totally different with a boy. There's no rush, and a man can always get married, but a girl has to be supported and she always has to think of that. My father says that she should stop pestering me. He says that it's smart of Erling to want to be a schoolteacher because they make good money and are never unemployed. 'White-collar workers,' says my brother, who fortunately has found work again, 'and they're the worst kind.' My brother is annoyed that I've got a boyfriend because he's always teased me that I'd never get married. He is listening to the news on the radio about Crown Prince Frederik's wedding, which greatly interests my mother. 'Turn off all that royalty junk,' says my father from deep in the sofa. 'Now we have one more mouth to feed, that's all.' At work, the office secretaries are completely ecstatic over the enchanting Crown Princess Ingrid. They take up one of their usual collections and walk through the stock room with a long list on which they write down what everyone donates for a bouquet for the royal house. I've given a krone, and a few days ago I gave a krone for the director's daughter's confirmation. He has so many children that there are constantly collections for their christenings or birthdays. 'Before you know it,' says Erling, 'your whole salary is used up for that nonsense.' Erling is a Social Democrat like my father and my brother, and he dreams of a revolution that will lift the masses. I like to hear him develop this plan, because it would further my own personal interests if the poor came to power. Erling wants to change the social democracy and make it more red. 'Actually,' he says, 'I'm a syndicalist.' I don't ask him what that is because then I'll get a long, incomprehensible speech about politics. Once he takes me along to a meeting at Blågårds Plads, but things get violent and the police take out their nightsticks and break up the brawling factions. 'Down with the cops,' yells Erling, who is in his DSU uniform, and immediately he gets a bop on the head that makes him give out a howl. Terrified, I grab him by the arm, and hand in hand we run down the street that echoes with the fleeing steps of the crowd. That's not for me and I never do it again. At work, besides us, there are two laborers and a driver. We all eat lunch together in a little room behind the stock room. It's not heated and that too, says Erling, is outrageous. As a rule, we all sit with our coats on. We sit on upside-down beer crates, and I get along well with this little group of people. I'm not shy with them – not even when they ask me, for example, if I really know what a truss or a vaginal syringe is used for. But I tell them that they should join the union, and one day when I'm in a light-hearted mood, I climb up on one of the beer crates and imitate Stauning when he speaks: 'Comrades!' I stroke my invisible beard and drop my voice to a low pitch, and my audience is very appreciative. They laugh and clap, and then I forget all about it. A little later, Mr Ottosen comes in and says that the director wants to speak to me. I haven't been alone with him since that day he grabbed my breasts, and I'm afraid that he wants something like that from me. 'Sit down,' he says curtly, pointing to a chair. I sit down on the very edge and, to my horror, I see that his face is dark with anger. 'We can't use you here,' he says hotly. 'I won't have Bolsheviks in my company.' 'No,' I say, not knowing what Bolsheviks are. He pounds the desk, so I jump. Then he gets up and comes over to my chair and sticks his red face right down into mine. I turn my head away a little because he has bad breath. 'You've urged my people to join the union,' he yells, 'but do you have any idea what would happen then?' 'No,' I whisper, even though I really do know. 'They'd be fired,' he roars and again pounds his hand on the desk, 'just like I'm firing you now – without a reference! You can pick up your check at the front office.' He straightens up and goes back to his place. I feel like I ought to burst into tears, but instead I'm filled with a dark joy that I can't define. This man regards me as dangerous, as significant in an area I know nothing about. 'There's nothing to laugh about,' he yells, so I must have been sitting there smiling. 'Get out!' He points to the door and I hurry to get out. 'I never want to see you again,' he screams after me and slams the door. Over in the stock room Mr Ottosen and Erling are looking astonished. They ask me what in the world is the matter and I tell them proudly. Mr Ottosen shrugs his shoulders. 'You're young,' he says, 'and badly paid, so you can easily find some other work to do. And you just have yourself, of course. I have a wife and four children, so I'll keep my mouth shut.' Erling says that I should have kept my opinions to myself, and I get furious with him. 'There'll never be a revolution here in Denmark,' I say hotly, 'as long as there are people like you that won't risk their own neck.' Then, indignantly, I go in to the secretaries and ask for my check, which is already waiting for me. The snow is piled high in the streets as I go home and an ice-cold wind whistles right through my coat. I've suffered for what I believe in, and I'm eager to tell my father about it. I feel like a Joan of Arc, a Charlotte Corday, a young woman who will inscribe her name in the history of the world. The poetry writing is going too slowly anyway. With straight back and head held high, I go up the stairs, and full of wounded dignity I step into the living room, where my father lies sleeping with his backside to the world. My mother asks me why I'm home already and when I tell her, she says that I shouldn't get involved in things that don't concern me. She says furiously that it was a good position and that no man will marry a girl who is constantly changing jobs. This time she doesn't back me up, and I clear my throat loudly and make a bit of racket at the table so my father will wake up.

And he does. When he sits up, rubbing his eyes, my mother says, 'Tove was thrown out. It's because of all your blabber about unions that she's gotten into her head.' When my father hears the details, his face takes on a furious expression. 'Who the hell do you think you are?' he yells, pounding his fist on the table so that the light fixture dances on its hooks. 'Here you've finally gotten a decent job and then you're thrown out for such foolishness. You don't know anything about politics. These are bad times and there are so many scabs that you could feed the pigs with them. But the next job you get you'll have to keep or else you'll be just like your mother.' They glare angrily at each other like they always do when there's trouble with Edvin or me. I keep quiet and really don't know what I had expected. But in the space of a few minutes, I've lost my suddenly awakened interest in politics, in red banners and revolutions. Erling and I go to the movies a few more Saturdays – then he stops leaning against the wall waiting for me. I miss him a little, because he made me less lonely, and I especially miss the attic with the metal boxes, where I wrote my first real poem. 'What's become of your young man?' asks my mother, who had dreamed of being mother-in-law to a schoolteacher. 'He found someone else,' I say. My mother has to have very concrete reasons for everything. She says, 'You should take more trouble with your appearance. You should buy a spring suit instead of that bicycle. When you're not nat-urally pretty,' she says, 'you have to help things out a bit.' My mother doesn't say such things to hurt me; she's just com-pletely ignorant of what goes on inside other people.

8

'Can you tell who I look like?' Miss Løngren is staring at me
with her bulging eyes, and I really can't see who she resembles. She smiles, raising and lowering her eyebrows. Maybe
she looks a little like Chaplin, but I don't dare say that, since
she's easily insulted. Now she's already frowning impatiently.
'Don't you ever go to the movies, young lady?' she says. 'Yes,
I do,' I say miserably and wrack my brain in vain. 'In profile,
then,' she says, turning her head. 'Now you can see it. Everyone says so.' Her profile doesn't tell me anything either other
than that she has a crooked nose and a weak chin. In the
middle of my ordeal, the phone rings. She takes it and says,
'I. P. Jensen.' She always says it in a high, threatening tone, so
I don't understand how the person on the other end dares
state their business. It's an order, and she writes it down,
holding the receiver at her right ear with her left hand. After
she has hung up, she says, 'Greta Garbo – now you can see,
can't you?' 'Oh yes,' I say, wishing I had someone to laugh
with. But I don't. In a strange way, I'm all alone here. I'm
employed in the office of a lithographer's shop. In the inner-
most room resides the owner, who is called Master. Whenever

he's in, his door is always closed. In the front office there are two desks. Carl Jensen, one of the sons, sits at one of them with his back to Miss Løngren's chair. She sits across from me by the telephone and the switchboard, and at the end of our desk there's a little table with a typewriter, which I'm supposed to learn to use. But all day long I have practically nothing to do, and no one seems to know why I was hired. There is an apartment upstairs above the offices, and this is where the other son, Sven Åge, lives. He is a lithographer and works across the courtyard in the print shop. Carl Jensen is thin and quick in his movements like a squirrel. He has brown, close-set eyes that are slightly crossed, which gives him a shifty appearance. He never speaks to me, and when he and Miss Løngren are both there, they act as if I were invisible. They flirt a lot with each other, and sometimes Carl Jensen turns in his chair, which can spin all the way around, and tries to kiss Miss Løngren. She swats at him and laughs loudly, flattered; I think it looks ridiculous because they're so old. Whenever Master goes through the office, they bend low over their work, and I quickly write down some figures or words that I afterwards slowly and carefully erase. Carl Jensen is not there very often, and I feel Miss Løngren's peering and attentive glance constantly resting on me. She comments on every move I make. 'Why are you always looking at the clock?' she says. 'It won't make the time go any faster.' She says, 'Don't you have a handkerchief? That sniffing is getting on my nerves.' Or, 'Why is it always me who has to get up to close the door? You're young, too.' The word 'too' astonishes me. One day she asks me how old I think she is. 'Forty,' I say cautiously, because I'm certain that she's at least fifty. 'I'm thirty-five,' she says, insulted, 'and people even say that I look younger than that.' Whenever I make an effort to be completely still and rest my gaze on a neutral spot, she says, 'Are you falling asleep? You've got to do *some* work for those fifty kroner that you get a month.' I happen to yawn, and she asks me with her manly voice whether I ever sleep at night. All day long I have to listen to these remarks and when I get home in the evening, I'm just as tired as when I was working at the boarding house. But I was the one who wanted to work in an office and I have to stay until I'm eighteen, even though it's a shocking thought. I enter the work orders in a book and I'm finished with that in an hour. Miss Løngren doesn't like me to practice on the typewriter because it makes such a racket. One day Master asks her timidly whether I could take care of the switchboard, and she says angrily that she doesn't want to sit with her back to the customers. Behind me there's a counter where the walk-in business takes place. Master seems to be just as afraid of her as I am. He's a heavy little man with a blue, spongy nose, which Miss Løngren says he didn't get for nothing. Whenever she has to find him, she always calls Grøften restaurant in Tivoli, which seems to be his permanent abode when he's not in his office. Once in a while he calls me in and gives me some slips of paper that I have to type up for him. They're letters and they all start with 'Dear brother' and are signed 'With fraternal greetings'. Sometimes they're about a brother who's passed away, and as I write about all of his magnificent qualities, especially in relation to the brothers, I can be quite moved, and I think there's a rare and beautiful closeness in that family. But one day when I venture to ask Miss Løngren how many brothers Master has, she breaks into loud laughter and says, 'They're his lodge brothers, all of them. He's a member of the Order of Saint George.' Afterwards, she tells the son about it and he turns his chair all the way around to see what such an idiot looks like. Every Friday evening I go around the print shop and hand out the pay envelopes. It's something of an ordeal because the workers make witty or fresh remarks to me, and I can't find a response right off the top of my head. I'm not one of them like in the nursing supply company. This job, my father says, is the best one I've had and I have no excuse for not staying there. Everyone is in the union – I am too. Master pays the dues, and I'm supposed to go to shorthand class, which Master will pay for too. I don't know why I'm supposed to learn shorthand since I'm only allowed to write to the brothers. Miss Løngren writes the invoices and the business letters. I get the impression that she was against hiring me and now is keeping me from learning anything at all. I sit and stare at her from eight in the morning until five in the evening, and it's hard and exhausting work. I've never met such a person before. Sometimes she's friendly and asks me, for example, whether I'd like an apple. She gives it to me, but when I crunch it in my mouth, she wrinkles her brow and says, 'Can't you even eat an apple without making a racket?' And if I visit the bathroom too often, she asks me whether I have indigestion. One day she says that her niece is going to be confirmed and she asks me whether I know anyone who could write a confirmation song. Just to surprise her, I say that I can, and she looks at me doubtfully. 'It has to be good,' she says, 'like the ones you read in the kiosk display windows.' I promise that it'll be good, and reluctantly she lets me try. I write the song to the required tune, 'The Happy Coppersmith', and Miss Løngren is impressed. 'It really is,' she says, 'just as good as the ones you pay money for.' She shows it to the son and he says to her, 'Well, I'll be damned', and 'you wouldn't have thought that of Miss Ditlevsen.' He turns his chair around and stares curiously at me with his shifty eyes. To me he doesn't say anything, as usual. 'Yes,' says Miss Løngren, 'something like that is a gift.' I find them both very stupid. Miss Løngren can't even speak correct Danish. For example, she says 'anyways' and she says it often. Whenever she wants to give her words emphasis, she says, 'I say, and I'll keep on saying, that . . .', etc. But naturally she doesn't keep on saying it. I have to spend two more years in this pointless way, and I find the thought almost unbearable. When I get home in the evening, Jytte is almost always there, and it wears me out listening to her and my mother talking. Jytte is big and blonde and pretty, and she herself says that she'll never get married because she so quickly tires of men. She's had a long series of lovers and is always entertaining my mother with stories about the latest one. They laugh a lot about it, and here too I feel myself left out. My father snores loudly and I can't go to bed until he leaves for work and Jytte has gone over to her own apartment. But I can't understand why I can barely tolerate people or how they ought to talk so that I'll listen willingly. They should talk the way Mr Krogh talked; when I'm walking in the street I always think that it's him turning the corner or cutting across the street. I run to catch up, but it's never him. They're in the process of putting up a new building where his once stood, and I never look in that direction when I go through the passage on my way home. I know that I could look him up in the telephone book, but my pride stops me. I didn't mean anything to him. I just amused him for a moment – then he shrugged his shoulders and turned his back. But I'm withering in this existence, and I've got to figure out something. I remember a column in the *Politiken* classified section headed 'Help Wanted: Theater and Music'. That would be something to do in the evening, and now I'm allowed to stay out until ten o'clock. Music is a closed realm for me, but I'd like to be an actress. In great secrecy I send in a reply to an ad looking for actors for an amateur theater. I get a letter from 'Succès Theater Company', which meets in a café on Amager, where I'm told to appear on a certain evening. I dress in my brown suit which, at my mother's insistence, I bought instead of the bicycle, and take the streetcar out to the restaurant. There I say hello to three serious young men and a young girl, who, like me, is there for the first time. We sit at a table and the leader says that he is thinking of putting on an amateur comedy called *Aunt Agnes*. He has the scripts with him, and after a short, appraising look, he decides that I'm to play Aunt Agnes. It is, he explains, a comic role that I'm wonderfully suited for. The woman is about seventy years old, but that can easily be taken care of with a little makeup. In the play, there's a young couple – the man will be played by himself and the girl by Miss Karstensen. I look over at the young girl and find her very beautiful. Her hair is platinum blond, her eyes deep blue, and her teeth white and perfect. I can easily see that I couldn't play her part. Still, I hadn't imagined my debut as a comic woman of seventy. When the roles are handed out and we've been ordered to meet again after we've learned our lines, we drink a cup of coffee and part. Miss Karstensen and I walk together to the streetcar. She asks if she may call me by my first name. Her name is Nina and she lives in Nørrebro. I ask her why she answered the ad. 'Because I was dying of boredom,' she says. She sways her hips a little as she walks, and I already feel happy in her company. Nina is eighteen and I'm sure that we're going to be friends.

9

The leader of our theater company is called Gammeltorv. He is twenty-two and has a wife and child. We rehearse at his house, and his wife is mad because the noise wakes up the baby. 'She doesn't have any feeling for art,' says Gammeltorv apologetically. But *he* does. When he directs us, he uses his head and arms and legs like famous conductors. He rages and yells at us and begs us, practically in tears, to put more soul into the lines and to throw ourselves totally into the roles. Aunt Agnes is a very silly and gullible person, constantly being made a fool of by the young couple; that's the comic part of the play, because the lines themselves are not funny. They are few and brief. The climax occurs when the woman comes into the living room with a tea tray in her hands. When she sees that the couple is sitting in a tight embrace on a love seat, she drops the tray, claps her hands, and says, 'God save us all!' When she says that, the hall is supposed to roar with laughter, says Gammeltorv, and I'm saying the words as if I were reading them out of a book! 'Again!' he roars. 'Again!' At last I succeed in putting enough astonishment into the lines, and he says that it will work when there are real cups on the tray. These his wife refuses to supply for me. At home in our living room, I act out Aunt Agnes for my mother, who is very enthusiastic. 'Maybe,' she says, 'you'll be a real actress. It's a shame that you can't sing.' Nina can – she has to trill a love-song duet with Gammeltorv, and in my opinion she does it very beautifully. The play is going to be performed in Stjernekroen on Amager, and Gammeltorv thinks there will be a full house because there's a dance afterwards. Nina and I are really looking forward to it. Nina is from Korsør, and her fiancé, who is a forester, lives there. He's coming to the opening. Nina works at *Berlingske Tidende* in the classified ad department, and she lives in a rented room in Nørrebro. It's a depressing and unheated room, where we sit on the edge of the bed with our coats on and confide our future plans to each other while we can hear the fire roaring in the family's stove on the other side of the thin wall. Some day Nina will marry her forester, because she wants to live her life in the country, but until that time she wants to have fun and enjoy her youth in Copenhagen. She says that when we're not so busy with the play anymore, we'll go to taverns and find someone to dance with. A girl can't sit in a pub alone, but when there are two, it's OK. I remember Mr Krogh's remark that people always want to use each other for something, and I'm glad that Nina has some use for me. Since I've met her, I don't think about Ruth as often. For that matter, she and her parents have moved away, so I never see her anymore when I come home in the evening. Nina grew up with her grandmother, who owns a hotel in Korsør. Her mother lives in Copenhagen with a man she's not married to. She is poor and cleans house for people; Nina says that some evening I should come home with her to meet her. My mother has no desire to meet Nina. 'Why does she live in Copenhagen,' she says, 'when her fiancé is in Korsør? Your girlfriends are always a bad influence.' At the office, Miss Løngren says sternly, 'You've been looking so happy lately. Has something nice happened at home?' I deny it, terrified, and try to look less glad. I'm taking a course in shorthand on Vester Voldgade, and it's lots of fun. Sometimes I think exclusively in shorthand symbols. One evening when I leave the office for home, Edvin is standing outside, looking very happy. As we walk home together, he tells me that soon he's going to marry a young girl whose name is Grete and who is from Vordingborg. They're going to be married in secret, and they've already found an apartment in Sydhavnen. I'm filled with a dark jealousy and have trouble sharing his enthusiasm. My mother and father are not to know until the wedding is over. 'They'll be furious,' I say, and feel a little sorry for them. 'You know Mother,' he just says, 'she freezes my girls out.' I tell him that on that point I'll have it easier, because my mother was delighted with Erling, even though she never got to meet him. He says that's the way it is most places, and there's nothing very strange about it. He asks how it's going with my poems and whether I will try another editor. 'They can't all die, you know.' I say that I've gradually begun to write better poems, but until I can do it well enough, I don't want to try again. But Edvin thinks that my children's poems are just as good as the ones you read in schoolbooks and newspapers, and I can't explain the indefinable difference between a good and a bad poem, because I've just recently found out myself. We stand there talking in front of the doorway at home for a little while as we stamp our feet to keep warm. Edvin doesn't want to come up with me because then my mother will suspect that we walked home together and she doesn't like us to have anything together that she's not part of. He hasn't gotten over his old grudge against my father for the four hard apprentice years, either. 'He's the one I can thank for my cough,' he says bitterly and a little unjustly. Edvin is twenty years old now, and around his jaw the skin is dark after shaving. His black curls fall over his forehead, and his brown eyes resemble my father's and Mr Krogh's. Some day I'll marry a man with brown eyes. Then maybe my children will have them too; I think I'll have the first one when I'm eighteen. Nina is completely horrified that I still have my virginity, and she thinks it's a defect that should be remedied as soon as possible. She says she was afraid too, because you hear so many things, but in reality it was wonderful. Nina has bought a long, slinky silk dress for the dance at Stjernekroen. It's cut low in the back, and she bought it on credit. It cost two hundred kroner, and I can't understand how she's ever going to pay for it. She laughs and says that of course she wasn't crazy enough to give her real name. I'm impressed – as always when someone dares to do something I don't. Over at Stjernekroen we're busy getting dressed and putting on makeup. I'm wearing Gammeltorv's grandmother's black dress. It reaches to the floor and underneath I have a pillow bound around my stomach. On my head I have a wig made of gray yarn, and Gammeltorv has drawn black lines on my face. They're supposed to be wrinkles. I have to walk bent over like a jackknife because I'm plagued by rheumatism in various places. We peek out through a hole in the curtain. We look down at our families and count to see if they're all there yet. They fill only the first three or four rows, and the rest of the hall is almost empty except for a few young people who are sitting, yawning, totally uninterested because they've only come for the sake of the dance. Nina shows me her forester, who is sitting right behind Aunt Rosalia. He looks like he's aloof from it all, but then Nina has told me that he's very much against her living in Copenhagen. 'What's he mad about?' asks Gammeltorv, who's looking with us. Then the band strikes up and the curtain lifts. My heart pounds violently from excitement, and I'm not sure that my Aunt Agnes will make anyone laugh. But it's an unusually receptive audience. They clap and enjoy themselves, and after every act Gammeltorv says that it can't help but be a success; have we seen that man writing on a notepad? That's a reporter from *Amagerbladet* and he's obviously been sent over because it's a big event. Finally the moment comes when, with the tray in my hands, I surprise the young folks on the love seat. I drop the tray, clap my hands, and cry out, 'God save us all!' At the same moment, a door is opened behind the stage entrance and the wig blows off my head. Horrified, I want to pick it up, but Gammeltorv shakes his head from the sofa because a hearty laughter swells up toward me from the hall. Laughter and clapping and stamping on the floor. Only Nina sends me an offended look because isn't *she* the star? When the curtain falls, Gammeltorv takes both my hands. 'You've saved the whole show,' he says, 'you'll have the leading role in the next play.' My family praises me too, and Edvin says that I have talent. He thinks he does too, but he's never had a chance. He dances with me a lot, and I'm grateful to him for that. He dances well, and Nina gives him a sidelong glance as she dances past with her forester. He's shorter than her and in general doesn't look like much. Edvin also dances with my mother and with both aunts, and at twelve o'clock my mother says that we have to go home, so I have to leave my friends. The next time we meet at the café on Strandlodsvej, Gammeltorv shows me a clipping from *Amagerbladet*, where, among other things, it says, 'A quite young girl, Tove Ditlefsen, was a great success as Aunt Agnes.' Even though my name is misspelled, it's a strange feeling to see it in print for the first time. 'And here,' says the enterprising Gammeltorv, 'are the scripts for the new play, *Trilby*. Trilby is a poor little girl who's in a magician's power. He forces her to sing and she sings beautifully.' 'And who,' says Nina coolly, 'is going to play Trilby?' 'Tove is,' he says, 'and since she can't sing, she just has to open and close her mouth. Then you stand in the wings and sing.' Nina gets red in the face with anger. She takes her purse and gets up. 'I won't have any part of it,' she says. 'You can sing yourself while she opens and shuts her mouth. I've had enough.' I stare at her, horror-stricken. 'I don't want any part of it, either,' I say. 'Nina is prettier than I am. So why should I play Trilby?' Suddenly we're all standing up. Gammeltorv pounds the table. 'Is it your theater company or mine?' he yells. 'Ha,' snorts Nina, 'Succès Theater Company! Any idiot can put an ad in a newspaper and pretend that he's somebody. I'm leaving!' 'Me too,' I yell, and rush out on her heels. I have to run to catch up with her. Suddenly we stand still, as if by mutual agreement. We're standing between two lampposts and the road is completely empty of people. There's a touch of spring in the air. Nina's narrow face wreathed with the fine halo of hair is still dark with anger, but suddenly she breaks into laughter and I do the same. 'So you were supposed to be the star,' she laughs. 'Oh, how funny.' We imagine how I was supposed to stand, opening and shutting my mouth without a sound coming over my lips while Nina sang with full voice, hidden from the audience. We laugh so we can hardly stop, and we agree that neither of us has talent for the theater. We'll have fun ourselves instead of entertaining others. We'll cut loose in the big, exciting city and find some young men we can fall in love with. Some young men who are nice to look at and who have money in their pockets. Now that we're not going to spend any more evenings with the idiotic rehearsals for *Aunt Agnes*, we have lots of time. The only tiresome thing about it is that I have to be home at ten o'clock, but for the time being there's nothing to be done about that.

IO

Aunt Rosalia is in the hospital. One day when my mother went out to visit her, Aunt Rosalia said, laughing, 'I'm young again, Alfrida.' My mother said that she should go to the doctor, but my aunt wouldn't. Like my mother, she only goes to the doctor under dire circumstances. My mother told me about it in the evening when I came home from the office. I didn't understand what the mysterious remark meant, but my mother explained that my aunt had started to bleed after it had stopped many years ago. Although my mother has never informed me about anything regarding those matters, she always assumes that I know all about it. But there were obviously gaps in the trash-can corner's sex education. It took my mother a long time to persuade my aunt to go to a doctor, and when she finally did, he put her in the hospital at once. Now she's going to have an operation, and she talks about it as if it were a picnic. 'It's cancer,' says my mother gloomily. 'First her husband – now her. And just when she was going to have some good years, now that she's gotten rid of that beast.' My mother is sincerely worried and unhappy about it, because she's much more fond of Aunt Rosalia than of Aunt Agnete. I visit her with my mother the day before the operation. She's lying there eating oranges and talking cheerfully with the other patients in the ward. I can't believe that my mother is right, because she doesn't look sick and she's not in pain. But when we've said goodbye and come out into the hallway, a nurse comes over and asks my mother who my aunt's nearest relatives are. When she hears that we are, she asks my mother to come in and talk to the doctor. In the meantime, I wait outside on a bench. My mother comes back with red eyes. She blows her nose loudly and leans on my arm as we leave. 'I thought so,' she sniffs. 'I was right. They don't know whether she'll survive the operation.' On the way to the office, I call Nina and say that I can't come over to her house that evening. I don't feel that I can leave my mother, and Jytte is no help when you're feeling bad about something. At the office, Miss Løngren says suspiciously, 'Well, so how was your aunt?' 'She has cancer,' I say solemnly, 'and she might die.' 'Well, well,' says Miss Løngren callously, 'we're all going to die, you know. Get to work now. Here are some letters.' I type letters to the brothers, and I've taken them in shorthand myself from Master's dictation. Carl Jensen comes in from the print shop and sits down in his revolving chair. He's wearing a gray smock and has a yellow pencil behind his ear. As far as I can see, he never does any work, but with Miss Løngren he doesn't have to pretend to do any, either. I can see that there's something he wants to say to her and that my presence is embarrassing him, but I calmly keep tapping at the typewriter, and I'm beginning to get faster at it. 'Løngren,' he says, leaning back so his face is close to hers, 'Sven Åge has his silver wedding anniversary in two weeks. Do you think it'd be possible to get someone to write a song for him?' His shifty eyes pass over me for a moment, but I don't look up. 'Oh God, yes,' says Miss Løngren, 'Miss Ditlevsen could, couldn't you?' The last words come loudly and shrilly and I don't dare pretend that I didn't hear them. 'Yes,' I say, addressing myself to Miss Løngren, 'sure I can.' 'Sure she can,' she says to Carl Jensen. 'She just needs some information, you know. What's happened through the years, things like that.' 'She'll have it,' says Carl Jensen, relieved. 'I'll bring it tomorrow.' I look at him sideways and suddenly I realize that it's a strange form of shyness that makes him unable to speak to me directly. That makes it less uncomfortable and puts the problem on his shoulders. The next day, I write the song while people walk past outside in the sunshine – independent people who can move about freely in the world between nine and five and who all have some personal goal that they've determined themselves. I write the ridiculous song while my aunt is being operated on and no one knows whether she'll survive. The telephone rings and Miss Løngren hands the receiver to me looking as if it's burning her fingers. 'It's for you,' she says sternly. 'It's a young woman.' Bright red in the face, I go around the desk and take the telephone as I stand close to Carl Jensen and Miss Løngren, who are completely silent. It's Nina, and I've forbidden her to call me. 'Hi,' she says. 'Just listen – I met a really sweet guy yesterday in the Heidelberg. He has a friend who's cute too. Tall, dark, and everything. You'll like him. I promised that we'd be there tonight. Then they'll both be there.' 'No,' I say in a low voice, 'I can't tonight. I have to be home.' 'Why?' she asks and, embarrassed, I whisper that I'll tell her some other time. I'm busy now. Nina is insulted and says that I'm strange. When she's finally found a young man for me, and I don't want to meet him. 'I've got to go,' I say. 'I'm busy. Goodbye.' Fumbling, I put down the receiver. 'Thank you,' I mumble, and go back to my place. 'Was that your girlfriend?' asks Miss Løngren after a long and oppressive silence. When I answer affirmatively, she says, 'She sounded rather frivolous. At your age, you have to be careful about the kind of girlfriends you have.' 'That's true,' says Carl Jensen, adding philosophically, 'In some ways, it's better to have a boyfriend – at least you know what's going on.' I keep working on the song, annoyed that there's nothing that rhymes with Sven Åge. Boa, Noah, protozoa, Balboa. Sven Åge is just as silent as his brother is talkative. He's fat like his father and his head is always tilted slightly, as if one neck muscle were too short. It gives him an endearing look. The brothers practically don't talk to each other at all because Sven Åge lives upstairs free of charge while Carl Jensen has to pay rent himself somewhere else. Furthermore, Sven Åge, as the oldest, is going to take over the press when Master dies. 'Sad,' says Miss Løngren sentimentally, 'that blood ties aren't stronger.' When I'm through with the song, I type it up on the typewriter, and when Master suddenly appears, I tear it out and stuff it away in the drawer because I'm not getting paid to write poetry for special occasions. When the product is done, I give it to Miss Løngren, and she's almost more enthusiastic than the time before. She stares at me as if I were a new Shakespeare and says, 'It's amazing – look here, Carl Jensen.' He takes the song and reads through it and agrees with her and stares at me for a long time without saying a word. Then he says to Miss Løngren, 'I wonder where she gets it from?' 'It's a gift,' determines Miss Løngren, 'a gift you're born with. I had an uncle who could do it, too. But it wore him out. It was as if all strength left him when he was done with a song. It's the same with mediums – they're completely exhausted by it, too. Aren't you tired, Miss Ditlevsen?' No, I'm not tired and my strength hasn't left me. But I want so badly to have a place where I can practice writing real poems. I'd like to have a room with four walls and a closed door. A room with a bed, a table and a chair, with a typewriter, or a pad of paper and a pencil, nothing more. Well, yes – a door I could lock. All of this I can't have until I'm eighteen and can move away from home. The attic with the metal boxes was the last place where I had peace. That and my childhood windowsill. I walk home, caressed by the soft May air. Now it stays light for a long time in the evening and I'm not cold in my brown suit. The jacket just reaches my waist and the skirt is pleated. I have a pleasant feeling of being well dressed when I wear it. Nina says I should have a bigger wardrobe, but I don't have any money. I pay twenty kroner a month at home now that I get all my meals there; ten kroner goes in the bank; and then there's twenty kroner left, a little less when medical insurance is paid for. Most of it I use for candy, because it's an inner battle to pass unscathed by a chocolate store. I also need money for the soda pop that I drink when I go to dance halls with Nina. The young men who might pay for it unfortunately don't show up until ten o'clock, when I have to say goodbye to the joys of nightlife. I think a little bit about what kind of young man Nina had chosen for me, and regret that I didn't get to meet him. But if my aunt is dead, I can't let my mother be alone. I always peek into baby buggies when I walk home, because I love to look at the little children who are lying asleep with upstretched hands on a ruffled pillowcase. I also like to look at people who in one way or another give expression to their feelings. I like to look at mothers caressing their children, and I willingly go a little out of my way in order to follow a young couple who are walking hand in hand and are openly in love. It gives me a wistful feeling of happiness and an indefinable hope for the future. Up in the living room my mother is sitting waiting for me. She's very pale and she has recently been crying. I'm fond of my mother, too, whenever she's prey to a simple and sincere emotion. 'She didn't die,' she says solemnly, 'but the doctor said that it's only a reprieve. The important thing now is that she doesn't find out what's wrong with her. Don't ever tell her.' 'I won't,' I say. My mother goes out to make coffee, and I look at my sleeping father's back. Suddenly I see that he is aged and tired. There's nothing definite to point to, it's just an impression that I get. My father is fifty-five years old, and I've never known him as young. My mother was first young, and then youthful, and she's still standing at that shaky stage. She lies without compunction that she's a couple of years younger, even to us, who know very well how old she is. She still gets her hair dyed and goes to the steambath once a week; these exertions fill me with a kind of compassion because they're an expression of a fear in her that I don't understand. I just observe it. When she puts the cups on the table, my father wakes up, rubs his eyes, and sits up. 'Have you told her?' he says grimly. 'No,' says my mother calmly, 'you can do it.' 'We've gotten a new apartment,' he says bitterly, 'over on Westend. It costs sixty kroner a month and I don't know where the money's going to come from when I'm unemployed again.' 'Nonsense,' says my mother harshly. 'Tove pays twenty, you know.' I'm horrified, because they shouldn't plan their future around my contribution. They shouldn't count on me in any way when they make plans behind my back. I ask them why they haven't told me before, and my mother says that they wanted to surprise me. There are three rooms and I'm to have one of them. And it looks out on the street so you can see what's going on. I feel a little happy after all, because I've always dreamed of having my own room. 'What the hell,' snaps my father, 'is she going to do in that room? Sit and bite her fingernails or pick her nose? Huh?' I get mad because he doesn't know anything about his own children. And whenever I get mad I always say something that I regret. 'I want to read,'

I say, 'and write.' He asks what in hell I want to write. 'Poems,'
I yell. 'I've written lots of poems and once there was an editor
who said they were excellent.' 'There, you see,' says my father,
rubbing his face with his big hand, 'she's crazy, too. Did you
know that she was fooling around with things like that?' 'No,'
says my mother curtly, 'but that's her own business. If she
wants to write, it's clear that she has to have her own room.' In
offended silence, my father takes his lunchbox and puts on his
jacket to go to work. When he puts on his cap, he stands there
a little, looking uncomfortable. 'Tove,' he says with a tender
voice, 'can I see your . . . uh . . . poems sometime? I know
something about that kind of thing.' My anger disappears completely. 'Yes, you can,' I say and he nods at me awkwardly
before he leaves. My father can regret and repent – an ability
that my mother doesn't possess. When he's left, she tells me
about the new apartment that we're going to move into on the
first. 'Three enormous rooms,' she says, 'that are almost like
ballrooms. It'll be nice to get away from this proletarian neighborhood.' When she's gone into the bedroom, I look around at
our little living room. I look at the old dusty puppet theater
that we were once so happy with when my father made it. It
will probably not survive a move. I look at the wallpaper that
bears various spots, many of whose origins I remember. I look
at the sailor's wife on the wall, at the brass coffee service on the
buffet, at the door handle that broke one time when my mother
slammed the door after her and that has never been repaired.
I look out the window over at the courtyard with the gas pump
and the gypsy wagon. I look at all this, which has remained
unchanged, and I realize that I detest changes. It's difficult to
keep a grasp on yourself when things around you change.

II

Summer is over and fall has come. The wildly colored leaves blow through the streets, and it's cold for me to go out in the brown suit. Since Edvin's made-over coat doesn't fit me anymore, I buy a coat on credit. It's totally against my father's advice. He says that you should pay everyone their due and make sure that you don't owe anyone anything, because otherwise you'll end up in Sundholm. We live on Westend now, on the ground floor, in number 32. My room is called the parlor whenever I don't take outright possession of it, and it's only separated from the dining room by a flowered cotton curtain. There's a table with crooked legs, two leather armchairs, and a leather sofa – all bought used and quite worn. I sleep on the sofa at night and its curved back makes it impossible for me to stretch out completely. 'Then maybe you won't grow much more,' says my mother hopefully. I myself often wonder how tall a person can continue to grow, but with me it doesn't seem to have any end. I'll soon be seventeen and I'm earning sixty kroner a month. My salary is according to union scale. I don't get much pleasure from my room because if I go in there in the evening, my mother yells through the curtain, 'What are you doing now? It's so quiet.' Usually I'm not doing anything other than reading my father's books, which I've already read. 'You can read just as well in here,' yells my mother in a voice as if heavy steel doors separated us. When she's in a good mood, she sticks her head in around the curtain and says, 'Are you writing poetry, Tove?' But usually I'm not home in the evening anymore, I go to the Lodberg or the Olympia or the Heidelberg with Nina, and we sit with our soda pop and watch the dancing couples in the middle of the floor – as if we haven't come there to dance ourselves. As a rule it's Nina who is chosen first. I smile at the young man who wants to dance with her, as if I were her mother, certain that now she's in good hands. I continue to smile approvingly as they dance past me, and I also look at other people in the room with interest. I imagine that people will think I'm studying my surroundings with the intention of writing a book about them sometime. For my sake, people can think what they like, just not that I'm an overlooked girl who's only out to get engaged. Once when I get up to dance with a young man who has taken pity on me, a man at the neighboring table mumbles, 'Even an ugly duckling can find a mate.' It ruins the whole evening for me. Nina says that it first gets to be fun after ten, and can't I get permission to stay out until twelve? But my mother won't hear of it. Nina also wants to fix me up a bit. Together we go out and buy a bra with cotton padding and a black and red cossack dress on credit. I don't dare tell them that at home, so I say I got it from Nina. These items help a good deal, to my astonishment, since I'm still the same person, whether I have cotton padding or not. 'The world wants to be fooled,' says Nina, satisfied, because she really wants me to be just as big a success as she is. One evening a handsome and serious young man asks me to dance. He's badly dressed, and while we dance, he tells me that the next day he's leaving for Spain to take part in the civil war. He lays his cheek against mine as we dance and even though it scratches a little, I like his caress. I lean a little closer to him and I can feel the warmth of his hand on the skin on my back. I get a little weak in the knees and feel something that I've never felt before at anyone's touch. Maybe he feels the same, because he stays standing with his arm around my waist until the music starts again. His name is Kurt and he asks if he can walk me home. 'You'll be the last girl I'm with before I leave,' he says. Kurt has been unemployed for three years and he would rather sacrifice his life for a great cause than rot in Denmark. He lives on welfare. When he was working, he was a driver for a taxicab owner, and he's never learned anything other than how to drive a car. He sits down at our table, and Nina smiles happily because I've finally found a young man I may be able to hold on to. We've agreed to keep away from unemployed young men, but it's hard to find one who's not. At ten o'clock, Kurt walks me home. It's clear moonlight and my heart is rather moved. I'm walking through the streets with a man who soon will suffer a hero's death. That makes him different in my eyes than all the others. His eyes are dark blue and almond-shaped, his hair black, and his mouth red like a small child's. At home in the entryway, he takes my head in his hands and kisses me very tenderly. He asks me if I live alone and I say no. He himself lives in a room with a vile landlady who doesn't let him have girls visiting. While we're standing embracing each other, my mother opens the window and yells, 'Tove, get up here now!' We jump apart terrified, and Kurt says, 'Was that your mother?' I can't deny it, and now we have to part. And Kurt has to go down by Trommesalen in order to get food from a sandwich store where it's handed out at midnight, but you have to get in line a couple of hours ahead of time. I stand watching him as he walks down the almost empty street. He's not wearing an overcoat and he has stuck both hands in the pockets of his jacket. He's going to die soon, and I'll never see him again. When I get upstairs, I make a scene over my mother's interference, but she says that I can just invite the young men up so she can see that there's nothing unsavory about them. She doesn't want me to go around with people who can't bear the light of day. And for that matter, she has other things to think about, because soon Aunt Rosalia is coming home from the hospital, where she's now been several times. She's coming home to us to die. That's what the doctors have told my mother. There's nothing more they can do, and there's no room in the hospital for people that the doctors can't do anything else for. Aunt Rosalia will lie in my father's side of the bed next to my mother. So my father will sleep on the sofa in the dining room. 'All of this,' says my mother, 'wouldn't have been possible in the old apartment', so it was as if an inner voice spoke to her when she begged my father to move.

One evening when I come home without a cavalier, I meet my father in the entryway. He's on his way out, as I'm going in. He looks enraged and bitter. 'Edvin's sitting up there,' he says. 'He's gotten married without saying a word to any of us. He's got a wife and apartment, and there's probably a kid on the way, too. Ha! – and him we've sacrificed so much for. Goodbye.' Before I let myself in (for now I have a key), I put on an astonished expression. 'Oh,' I say, 'are you here?' They're sitting in my room because Edvin is a guest now, and that's what you use a parlor for. My mother is bawling and Edvin looks very ill at ease. Maybe he regrets his pig-headedness, which also seems to me a little extreme. 'It was to surprise you,' he says meekly, 'and so you wouldn't have the expense of the wedding.' That only makes matters worse. My mother asks, offended, whether he thinks they couldn't afford a little wedding present, 'but I suppose we're just not fine enough.' Then Edvin shows us a picture of his wife. Her name is Grete and she has a round face with dimples. My mother studies it with a frown. 'Can she cook?' she asks and stops crying. Edvin has no idea. 'She doesn't look like she can,' says my mother. My mother herself is no great shakes in the kitchen, and everything edible that she makes has a cementlike consistency because she digs too deeply into the flour bag. While we drink coffee and eat pastry, she asks how much Edvin's rent is and whether his wife is going to work as long as there aren't any children. She's not, and my mother wonders how she'll manage to pass the time. It's very clear that she's already formed an unfavorable opinion of Grete that won't change for the better through personal acquaintance. The clock strikes eleven in the dining room and Edvin gets up to go. 'We'll come on Sunday, then,' he says dejectedly. When he's left, my mother wants to talk, and I want to be alone. I want to be alone to think about Kurt, and I want to write down some lines that came to me as I watched him go down the street without once turning around. At the corner of Westend and Matthæusgade there's a tavern where a band by the name of 'Bing and Bang' blares until two in the morning. Because of that, we practically have to shout at each other; it was far quieter in the old apartment. My mother asks me what kind of a young man I was standing there kissing. 'One I danced with,' I say. 'Other than that I don't know.' She says that I should always make a date before the young men leave. She suffers from a nagging fear that I'll never get engaged, and is prepared to receive any young man royally if he's just the least bit interested in me. 'You're too critical,' she says point-blank. 'You can't afford to be that way.' Finally she leaves and I sit down at the table with the crooked legs and take out paper and pencil. I think about the handsome young man who's going to die in Spain and then I write a poem that is good. It's called 'To My Dead Child' and has no obvious connection with Kurt. Still, I wouldn't have written it if I hadn't met him. When it's done, I'm no longer sorry that I'll never see him again. I'm happy and relieved and yet melancholy. It's so sad that I can't show the poem to a living soul and that everything still has to wait until I meet a person like Mr Krogh. I've shown Nina my poems and she thinks they're all good. I've shown my father the poem I wrote in the attic with the metal boxes, and he said that it was an amateur poem and that things like that were a good hobby for me – like when he did crossword puzzles. 'You train your brain with things like that,' he said. I can't explain to myself, either, why I want so badly to have my poems published, so other people who have a feeling for poetry can enjoy them. But that's what I want. That's what I, by dark and twisting roads, am working toward. That's what gives me the strength to get up every day, to go to the printing office and sit across from Miss Løngren's Argus eyes for eight hours. That's why I want to move away from home the same day I turn eighteen. Bing and Bang roars through the night; drunk people are thrown out into our courtyard from the café's back door. There they yell, swear, and fight, and not until morning is there silence in the courtyard and on our street.

I2

Rumors of my poetic abilities have reached the print shop, and now orders come in every day. Carl Jensen receives them and brings them to Miss Løngren, who is still the only one I stand in direct contact with. I write songs for all kinds of occasions and when I go over to hand out the pay envelopes, the workers thank me, embarrassed, and just as embarrassed, I say that there's nothing to thank me for. I write songs and in shorthand I take important messages to the brothers or obituaries of dead brothers. They're printed in the Order of Saint George newsletter. All of this doesn't have much to do with office work, but Miss Løngren won't train me; when she was on vacation, everything was on the verge of collapse because I didn't know the first thing about anything. When I turn eighteen, I'll apply for a real office job and no longer work as a trainee. Then I can get a much higher salary. When I turn eighteen the world will be different in every way, and Nina and I will have the whole night at our disposal. Then I'll also have to see about getting rid of my virtue – Nina is very set on that. She herself was only fifteen when the forester took hers. Whenever we go out in the evening, she takes off her engagement ring. She only goes to bed with those young men who are not unemployed, and I haven't told her about Kurt. That's an experience I want to keep for myself. If I had lived in a room, I would have taken him in. But I don't know whether I would have taken in other young men who have walked me home and kissed me in the entryway. One day when Nina is pressuring me again because of my scandalous virginity, I tell her that I want to be engaged first. That's not something that I've thought about before, but the decision relieves me. In reality there has only been one real prospective buyer for my virtue, and it's a little embarrassing, because Nina talks as if everyone is out after it. Now that Aunt Rosalia is lying at home sick, my mother is a lot less concerned with what I'm doing. All day she sits in there by my aunt's bed, talking and laughing, and in the evening she goes to bed early and lies there, talking on until one of them falls asleep. My father has become totally superfluous in her world, and I think she would be completely happy if my aunt wasn't going to die. My aunt is yellow in the face and her skin is so stretched over her bones that you're continually reminded of her skull's existence. Her skin is so tight that she can't even close her mouth all the way anymore. If she's awake in the evening when I come home, she calls me in and I sit down by her bed for a while. I try to hold my breath the whole time because there's a terrible smell around the bed, and I hope that my aunt doesn't notice it herself. When she's in pain, my mother phones from the café on the corner for a nurse, who comes and gives her an injection of morphine. It makes her hazy, and she often mistakes my mother and me for each other. 'I'm going to die, Alfrida,' she says to me one evening. 'I know it. You don't have to hide it from me.' 'No,' I say unhappily, 'you're just sick. The doctor says you'll be well soon.' 'It was the same with Carl,' she says. 'The doctor said that I shouldn't tell him.' I don't answer, just put her emaciated hands underneath the comforter, turn off the light, and go into my own room where I can hear my father's snoring through the cotton curtain. I would have liked to speak honestly with my aunt because I'm sure that it would have made her happy, but I don't dare because of my mother, who acts out her sad comedy while my aunt pretends that she doesn't know anything. I think that I would want to know the truth when I'm going to die someday. I also think that if I meet a young man I like, I can't invite him up, as my mother always requests, because the smell from my aunt fills the whole apartment. We've all been out to Sydhavnen to visit my brother and his wife. They have a two-room apartment with a few pieces of furniture that were bought on credit, which made my father put on a foreboding expression. Grete is tiny and plump and smiling, and she sat on Edvin's lap the whole time, while my mother looked at her as if she were a vampire who would suck all strength out of him before long. She hardly spoke to her, and conversation was difficult, too, since my mother carefully avoided addressing her directly. I'm so tired of my family because it's as if I run up against them every time I want to move freely. Maybe I can't be free of them until I get married myself and start my own family. One evening when we're sitting in the Lodberg over our soda pop, a young man asks Nina to dance and steps onto the dance floor with her, and I sit as usual with my maternal smile, watching youth amuse itself. Then a young man bows before me and we step out onto the crowded dance floor. He hums in my ear to the music, 'The young man from Rome, don't count him out.' 'That's Mussolini,' I say. I happen to know that because my brother was outraged by the song that Liva Weel often sings. 'Who's that?' asks the young man, and I say that I don't know. I only know that it's a man in Italy who's just like Hitler, and that you shouldn't write Danish songs that praise him. 'Your girlfriend is dancing with my friend,' he says. 'His name is Egon. And I'm Aksel. What's your name?' 'Tove,' I say. Aksel dances well and he's in no way fresh during the dance like most of them. 'You dance well,' he says, 'better than most of the girls.' I tell him that I've never learned to dance and he says that it doesn't matter. I have rhythm in my body. It's very rare that any of the young men say anything while you dance with them, and I like Aksel. We dance past Nina and Egon; I smile at Nina, and Egon and Aksel say hi to each other. When the music stops, Aksel asks if they can sit at our table and I say yes. Nina's beautiful eyes shine with happiness when we reach our table. She asks, 'Don't you think Egon is handsome?' and I say, 'Yes, I do.' 'He's a carpenter,' she says, 'and he lives in a house on Amager with his parents, and Aksel lives across the street with his parents. In a house too.' Then they come over and sit down and I look closer at Aksel. He has a round, friendly face and everything about him reminds you that he was once a child. The light curly hair is a little damp on his forehead, the blue eyes have a trusting expression, and he has a deep cleft in his chin, which is only erased when he laughs. There's a faint scent of milk about him. Egon is shorter than he is, dark, and apparently somewhat older. Nina asks him how many rooms there are in his house, and I can see that she's far away in a dream about two rich men's sons who will lift up two poor girls into their carefree world. Maybe she's even considering giving the forester the sack. I have the impression that he's heavy and serious, and that Nina has a much too romantic picture of the future he'll provide for her in the country. When she's being very silly she calls him The Shrub, but no one else is allowed to. She's with him every weekend and I'm not permitted to meet him. He's not allowed to meet me, either, because she thinks that he'll think I'm a bad influence, like my mother thinks Nina is a bad influence on me. 'And what do you do?' Nina asks Aksel as we drink the beers we ordered. 'I'm a collection agent,' he says, smiling charmingly at her. I don't know what that is, but Nina looks disappointed. 'Oh,' she says, 'you go around with bills and things like that?' 'Drive,' he corrects her with a certain conceitedness. 'I drive a van.' Her face brightens a little and suddenly she suggests that we all celebrate our meeting. We drink to that, and I would much rather have had a soda pop. I don't like beer. Since it's past ten, I admit dispiritedly that I'll have to leave. Aksel jumps up gallantly and buttons his jacket, which is very broad across the shoulders. He's tall and extraordinarily knock-kneed. He takes me easily by the arm as we walk across the room together, and out in the cloakroom he helps me with my coat. As we walk through the cool streets, where the city's lights outshine the stars, he tells me that he's an adopted child and that his parents are quite old, but very nice. And to my astonishment, he asks me whether I feel like coming over to meet them someday. 'Sure,' I say. 'I want so much to have a steady girlfriend,' he says childishly and forthrightly. 'And the old folks want me so badly to get engaged.' At home in the entryway he kisses me according to program, but I can tell that he doesn't feel anything special by it, not even when I press myself lovingly against him. He says, 'The four of us can have fun together.' 'Yes,' I say, and promise to come out to visit him next Sunday. He asks curiously if I'm a virgin and I admit that I am. He grabs my hand and shakes it heartily. 'I respect that,' he says warmly. Disappointed and confused, I go to bed. I think about whether you can get engaged to a collection agent. I have a suspicion that it's just a nicer expression for bicycle messenger, except that he drives a van.

13

Aksel and I are formally engaged after knowing each other for two weeks, and treating each other as chastely as if we were brother and sister. Nina told Egon that I wouldn't go to bed with Aksel until we were engaged, and Egon told Aksel, who suggested the engagement as his own spontaneous idea. Now I'm an engaged girl, and my mother is thrilled. She thinks Aksel looks stable; just as she could tell that Edvin's wife couldn't cook, she can tell that Aksel doesn't drink. He behaves very gallantly toward my mother. 'Anyone can see,' she says to my father, who doesn't contradict her, 'that he's an educated person.' After spending several evenings with him, my father says, 'You know, he's never learned anything except how to drive a car.' 'Well,' says my mother offended, 'isn't that good enough? Maybe you know how to drive a car?' Aksel has promised to take my mother out driving someday; I don't give it much thought, however. But one day, while I'm innocently sitting in the office, there is a loud honking outside and Miss Løngren stares out the window. 'Who on earth is that?' she says astonished. 'They're waving over here. Is it someone you know?' I deny it, blushing, because Aksel and my mother are waving like mad and leaning out the window while Aksel honks the horn, long and rhythmically. 'It must be for the people upstairs,' I say miserably. 'What nerve,' says Miss Løngren, drawing the curtains tighter together. When I get home, I say furiously that I don't want any part of that stupid waving, and my mother says that she and Aksel had so much fun all day. They went to a pastry shop and Aksel treated her. Her eyes shine, as if she were the one who was engaged to him. Aksel's parents are both tiny and old and tremendously nice. They live in a bungalow in Kastrup. The father is a foreman in a factory and there's an air of affluence over the house. Aksel has his room down in the basement. He has a radio and a phonograph and over three hundred records, arranged on tall shelves like books. The room next door is a billiard room where all four of us play billiards when Nina and Egon are there. Aksel's parents call him Assemand and treat him as if he were a little boy. He's very loving toward them just as he is toward me. He has a warmth in his being that makes you feel secure and comfortable. One day Nina says that we're going to have a little party out at Aksel's. We're going to drink his father's homemade wine and we've gotten permission for this from Aksel's parents. We're also going to dance and play billiards and afterwards I must give Aksel the great pleasure of going to bed with him. 'When you've been drinking,' says Nina encouragingly, 'it doesn't hurt a bit.' Egon also thinks it's about time, Nina tells me, and it's really as if Aksel and I aren't even consulted. We don't talk about it at all and he still respects me to a fault. Nina and I go out there together and Aksel is a conscientious host. He opens the bottles and puts on records and we all get giddy from the wine, which doesn't taste nearly as terrible as beer. Egon sits and kisses Nina in between dances. She laughs and says if only The Shrub could see this, because she's told her secret to Egon, who makes fun of The Shrub, whom he imagines sitting on the doorstep, tamping his evening pipe as he watches the sunset. We all laugh loudly at this stereotype. 'Nina comes out,' elaborates Egon, encouraged by his success, 'with three sniveling kids hanging on to her dress, dries her hands on her apron and says, "Papa, it's time for evening coffee." ' Aksel doesn't kiss me at all and as time goes on, he grows more and more serious. I almost feel sorry for him because in so many ways he seems like a child. I myself have gotten very animated from the wine and I'm really set on going through with it now. It surely won't be any worse for me than for so many others. Sometime after midnight, Nina and Egon sneak into the billiard room and close the door behind them. 'What are you doing in there?' Aksel yells unnecessarily. Then he looks at me, uncertain and afraid. 'Well,' he says, 'I'd better make the bed.' He does this with slow, careful movements. 'Take off your clothes,' he says miserably, 'at least some of them.' It's like being at the doctor's. 'Why don't we talk a little first?' I ask. 'Sure,' he says and we sit down in separate chairs. He fills our glasses to the top and we empty them greedily. 'You should see about getting your front teeth filled,' he says gently. 'Yes,' I say astonished. Unlike the other procedure, though, it costs money to go the dentist. 'I can't afford it,' I add. Then he offers to pay for it and since I don't feel that I can accept, he says that he's going to support me someday anyway. So I thank him and agree to let him pay for the fillings. 'It's a shame,' he explains, 'because otherwise you're so pretty.' Suddenly there's a strange howl from the billiard room, and both of us gasp. 'It's Egon,' explains Aksel. 'He's so passionate.' 'Are you too?' I ask cautiously, because I'd like to be prepared for it if he's actually going to roar. 'No,' he says honestly, 'I'm not very passionate.' 'I don't think I am either,' I admit. A glimmer of hope appears in his eyes. 'We could,' he says optimistically, 'wait until another time?' 'Then they'll think we're crazy,' I say, nodding toward the billiard room. 'No. Well, we could turn out the light.' Aksel turns out the light. I clench my teeth and lie listening to his warm, kind, reassuring words. The whole thing isn't so bad, and he doesn't utter any animal-like sounds. Afterwards he turns on the light again, and we both laugh with great relief that it's over and that it wasn't anything special. 'I want to tell you,' he confesses, 'I've never been to bed with a virgin before.' Nina and Egon appear in the door with flushed cheeks and shining eyes. They look from the bed to us and then at each other, as if it were all their doing, but nothing is said about it. We continue dancing, because when I'm with Aksel, I'm allowed to come home late. With him I can do anything, so this wouldn't upset my mother, either, if she found out. Later Nina asks me if it wasn't wonderful, and of course I say yes. She says that it gets better and better each time. I hadn't considered that the procedure would be repeated. In reality I think that it was a completely insignificant event in my life – not nearly as important as my brief meeting with Kurt and what that meeting could have developed into. But still, I write in my diary that I've kept since I got my own room, 'As Nina gave herself to Egon with all of her warm, passionate body in the billiard room, I answered Aksel's question about whether I was innocent with a pure and chaste "yes," etc.' In my diary everything is sheer romanticism. I store it in the top dresser drawer in the bedroom at home. I've had an extra key made for it. In the drawer are also my two 'real' poems, three thermometers, and five or six condoms. The latter items I stole from the nursing supply company because at one time I thought of opening a nursing supply store. But I was thrown out before my stock was large enough. To my great relief, Aksel continues to treat me exactly as before, and he never refers to the embarrassing interlude. I think that he does everything that Egon tells him to do, just as I tend to do whatever Nina wants me to. When I'm alone with Nina, I pretend that Aksel and I are frequently together and maybe he does the same when he's with Egon. During the day Aksel drives around with my mother, who sits in the delivery van and waits while he's with customers. He works for a furniture company, and he tells me that there are many whores among the customers. My suspicious mother has discovered that he stays an especially long time with them, but he just says that it's difficult to get the money from them. My mother says that I shouldn't trust him, but actually I couldn't care less whether he goes to bed with the whores. I don't think it's any concern of mine or my mother's. It's worse that I sense a certain coolness from his parents whenever I'm visiting. I can't figure out how I've offended them. Once in a while I catch his mother staring at me sharply when she doesn't think I'll notice. She's very tiny and always dressed in black like my grandmother. She has wise brown eyes and completely white hair. I've never seen her without an apron. 'Has Aksel promised to pay your dentist bill?' she says one evening. 'Yes,' I say, feeling uncomfortable. 'He doesn't make very much,' says his mother. 'I'm afraid that you may have to pay it yourself.' There's something that I don't understand at all. One evening when I'm invited to dinner, I get there a little before Aksel. His parents look very serious. His mother says that Aksel isn't the man for me. He'll never be able to support a wife, and I'm too good for him. 'Let me,' says his father, waving at her with his hand. 'The thing is,' he says, 'many times we've paid the company back when there've been funds missing. I mean, when Aksel has taken money that isn't his. When it comes to money, he's a child. We thought it would help when he got engaged to a nice girl, but it hasn't helped. He's our only son and our greatest sorrow. He's run away from eleven apprenticeships, and the only things he thinks about are cars and records.' 'He's a good boy,' his mother defends him, wiping her eyes, 'but reckless and irresponsible.' 'I like him a lot,' I say. 'And I don't need to be supported. I can make a living writing poetry.' The latter slips out of me involuntarily and I look at Aksel's parents, horrified. They don't look very surprised. 'I knew you weren't an ordinary young girl. You can see that,' says his mother. Then Aksel drives up and stops out in the gravel with screeching brakes. He often drives home in the company van. As he rings the bell, his mother says, 'Now you can't say that you weren't warned.' I think it over for a few days and am very glad that people can see I'm not ordinary. It wasn't so many years ago that I was unhappy about that. I think a lot about my fiancé and I reach the conclusion that he's not suited to be a lifelong mate to a girl who wants to break into high society someday. But I can't get myself to break the engagement. I feel sorry for Aksel, who is still gallant and kind and respects me. But my mother also starts to wonder why Aksel always has money in his pocket and why he stays so long with the whores. She stops accompanying him in his van and she advises me to see about finding someone else, someone like Erling who wanted to be a schoolteacher, whom I spurned as if there were a whole line of young men waiting at my door. Nina is in the midst of a serious crisis, because she's considering breaking off with The Shrub and marrying Egon. When I tell her what I know about Aksel, she advises me to end things with him as soon as my dental work is done. The fillings are almost invisible, and when they're finished, Nina thinks that I can get whoever I want. She says that I've finally gotten some 'class', and that's what men notice. But I'm so happy when I'm with Aksel because I'm really fond of him. I'm happy and secure in his company. I stop visiting his parents, and he stops visiting mine. My mother treats him coldly now and my father asks him questions that only serve to show his ignorance. 'What do you think about the Olympics? Huh? Isn't it scandalous?' my father says to him. He means the Olympics in Berlin where our girl swimmers are, but Aksel knows nothing about any Olympics. He only knows a little about Hitler and the world situation, and he hasn't read *The Last Civilian* by Ernst Glaeser. I have, and so I know a lot about the persecution of the Jews and the concentration camps, and all of it fills me with fear. It's so pleasant with Aksel because he knows nothing about all the things that could terrify a person these days. That doesn't mean that he's an idiot, but my father's interrogation is only aimed at showing that he is. He senses that and stops visiting. So we're homeless when we're together and only have the taverns and the streets. One day he picks me up outside the office, and silently, we walk down H. C. Ørstedsvej. It's clear that there's something he wants to tell me. Finally it comes. 'I've been thinking,' he says, 'that we ought to take off our rings. I've never really been in love with you.' 'And I haven't been in love with you, either,' I say. 'No,' he says, 'I know that.' He takes great strides, out of sheer embarrassment, and I have to jog to keep up with him. 'And I'll be eighteen soon,' I say, not knowing what that has to do with anything. 'Yes,' he says, 'then you won't be a minor anymore.' We walk for a while without saying anything. 'And my mother says you're too good for me,' he explains. 'You should marry someone who has a lot of money and reads books and things like that.' 'Yes,' I say, 'I think so too.' At home in the entryway, he kisses me tenderly as always and then twists the ring off his finger. He puts it in his pocket and mine goes there too. 'Maybe,' he says, 'we'll see each other again.' His short, stiff eyelashes scratch my cheek for the last time. Then he walks down Westend with his scissors-shaped legs and his supple boy's back. He turns around and waves at me. 'Bye,' he yells. 'Bye,' I yell back, waving. Then I go up, taking a deep breath before I put the key in the door, because the smell is getting worse and worse. I go in to my mother and Aunt Rosalia. 'Now I'm not engaged anymore,' I say. 'That's fine,' says my mother. 'He wasn't much good.' 'Yes, he was,' I say and then keep quiet. I can't explain to my mother what was good about Aksel. 'There's something good about everyone, Alfrida,' says my aunt gently from her bed. And we both know she's thinking about Uncle Carl.

14

One morning when I turn the corner onto the road in Frederiksberg where the printer's is located, I see that the flag is at half-mast in the little front yard of the office building. My first thought is that perhaps it's Miss Løngren who is dead, which fills me with perverse glee. Then I'll be allowed to mind the switchboard and talk on the telephone. And I can call Nina as often as I like. In a rather good mood, I go up the stairs, but when I step in the door, Miss Løngren is sitting at her usual place and blowing her nose with a great blast. It's all red, as if she's been sitting in the hot sun. 'Master is dead,' she says with a breaking voice, 'quite suddenly. He was with the brothers at the lodge. In the middle of a speech he fell over the table. A heart attack – there was nothing to be done.' I sit down at my place and say nothing. Master was a very taciturn man that everyone was afraid of, even his sons. He had difficulty expressing himself in writing, and I always embellished the language in the letters to the brothers and in the obituaries, because he couldn't remember what he had dictated. Aside from dictating letters, he'd never spoken to me. Miss Løngren stares at me reproachfully while I enter the work lists.

'You could at least offer your condolences,' she says. 'What's that?' I ask. She doesn't condescend to give an explanation, but continues her reading of the newspapers. 'Did you hear King Edward's abdication speech?' she asks. 'It was gripping. To give up a throne for the sake of a woman! And he's so handsome. Princess Ingrid didn't get her hands on him after all.' 'He looks like Leslie Howard,' I venture to say, and now it's her turn to ask who's that. She shows me a picture of Mrs Simpson and says, 'It's just so strange that he would fall in love with such a middle-aged woman. I could understand it better if it had been a young girl.' She runs her fingers through her old-maid hairdo, as if the thought crosses her mind that the world would have better understood it if it had been for her sake. 'He was handsome when he was young,' she says dreamily, meaning suddenly Master. 'Carl Jensen looks like him, don't you think? I'll buy a black suit for the funeral – I owe him that. What are you going to wear? Well, you can wear your suit, since it's spring.' The death and the abdication have made her talkative. She says that there will certainly be big changes now, and these changes will probably mean that I'll be let go. It was completely Master's idea that I was hired at all. These bright prospects fill me with joy and comfort. There's only half a year until I turn eighteen and it's about time that I move out. In every way the air is too thick to breathe.

Aunt Rosalia doesn't have long to live, and the light-hearted conversations with my mother have stopped completely. My aunt is unable to eat and she is in a lot of pain. My father tiptoes around like a criminal because my mother snaps at him as soon as she sets eyes on him. Edvin and Grete still haven't been to visit us because my mother doesn't have the energy for housekeeping chores in her sorrow-laden condition. She sleeps very little at night, so I've gotten myself an alarm clock and make coffee myself in the morning. Every evening I'm with Nina, who – after an inner battle – has broken off the relationship with Egon because she'd rather live in the country with The Shrub. And almost every night, when the taverns have closed, I stand downstairs in the entryway kissing some young man who's usually unemployed and who I never see again. After a while I can't tell one young man from the next. But I've begun to long for the intimate closeness with another human being that is called love. I long for love without knowing what it is. I think that I'll find it when I no longer live at home. And the man I love will be different from anyone else. When I think about Mr Krogh, I don't even think that he needs to be young. He doesn't have to be particularly handsome, either. But he has to like poems and he has to be able to advise me as to what I should do with mine. When I've said goodbye to the night's young man, I write love poems in my diary, which has taken the place of my childhood poetry album. Some of them are good and some of them are not so good. I've learned to tell the difference. But I don't read many poems anymore, because then I easily end up writing something that resembles them. Master's funeral is a terrible trial for me. Carl Jensen gives a speech out in the cemetery for both the workers and the family. The wind carries the words in the other direction and I don't hear any of them. I stand behind the youngest and most insignificant of the personnel, and next to me is a delicatessen worker who is very pregnant. It starts raining and I'm freezing in my suit. Suddenly the thought strikes me that I could be pregnant, and it's odd that I haven't thought of that before. Aksel apparently didn't think of it either. How do you know if you're pregnant? Suddenly I think that there are all kinds of signs that I am, and if it's true, I don't know what I'm going to do. Nina has confided to me that she can't have children; otherwise she would have gotten pregnant long ago. She says that the young men never use anything; they couldn't care less. I think about my mother, who always says that I can't come home with a kid, but I especially think about how it will hinder me in my vague wandering toward an equally vague goal. I would like very much to have a baby, but not yet. Things must come in the proper order. When the speech is over and everyone is going over to drink coffee or beer, I tell Miss Løngren that I have to go home because my aunt is about to die. She looks like she doesn't believe me, but I don't care. I rush home and look at myself in the mirror in the hallway. I think I look bad. I feel my breasts and imagine they're tender. I think about cream puffs and imagine I feel nauseous. I smooth my hand over my flat stomach and imagine it's gotten bigger. At five o'clock I'm standing in Pilestræde, outside *Berlingske Tidende*, waiting for Nina. I confide my fear to her and she says that I should go to the doctor. The next day I stay home from work and go up to old, mean Dr Bonnesen; with difficulty I manage to blurt out my errand. 'You knew very well what could happen,' he snaps in a harassed tone, 'before you started these highjinks.' He gives me a urine bottle and the next morning I deliver it full. The next few days Miss Løngren asks me where my thoughts are, since I'm not listening to what is said to me. Her own thoughts are still jumping from Master to the Duke of Windsor and back again. I feel her searching glance on me like a physical pain and fervently hope for the promised layoff. Several days later I finally find out that I'm not pregnant, and I'm filled with enormous relief. 'I'm very romantic,' confesses Miss Løngren as she pages through a magazine full of pictures of the world's most celebrated couple. 'That's why I can cry over something like this. Can't you? Aren't you at all romantic?' Such questions always contain a lurking reproach, and I hurry to assure her that I'm very romantic. The word makes me think of dark Bedouins with scimitars, of moon-lit nights by the river, of dark blue, star-filled nights. I think of loneliness and the complete lack of family or relatives, of a garret room with a candlestick and a pen scratching across the paper, and of a man whose face and name are hidden from me for the time being. 'Yes,' says Miss Løngren thoughtfully, 'I think you are, too. Otherwise you wouldn't be able to write such beautiful songs.' She also says, 'Why don't you set your-self up as a freelance poet? You could earn a lot of money at it.' I think for a moment that I could have a sign in the window at home: 'Songs composed for all occasions.' And then my name underneath. But my mother probably wouldn't want a sign like that in the window.

One night shortly after Master's funeral, my mother wakes me up. 'Come,' she says, 'I think it's about to happen.' Her face is totally unrecognizable from crying. My aunt has tensed her body into an arc and cast her head back so the hard sinews of her neck look like thick ropes under the yellow skin. Her throat rattles eerily and my mother whispers that she's unconscious. But her eyes are open and roll around in their sockets as if they want to get out of them. My mother says that I should go and call the doctor. I dress quickly and borrow the telephone in the café on the corner where Bing and Bang play noisily in the back-ground. The doctor is a kind man who stands for a long time, looking sadly at my aunt. 'Should she be given the last one?' he says as if to himself as he draws the syringe. 'Yes,' pleads my mother, 'it's terrible to see her suffer like this.' 'All right.' He injects her in her bony leg and a little later all of her mus-cles relax. Her eyes close and she lies back and starts to snore. 'Thank you,' says my mother to the doctor, following him out without thinking about her wrinkled nightgown. Then we sit together by the deathbed and neither one of us thinks of

waking my father. Aunt Rosalia is ours and only a minor char-
acter in his life. Late into the night, my aunt stops snoring and
my mother puts her ear to her mouth to see if she's breath-
ing. 'It's over,' she says. 'Thank God she found peace.' She sits
back on the chair again and gives me a helpless look. I feel very
sorry for her and I feel that I ought to caress her or kiss her –
something completely impossible. I can't even cry when she's
looking at me, although I know that someday she'll say that I
didn't even cry when my aunt died. She'll mention it as a sign of
my heartlessness and maybe it will happen when I move away
from home soon. I've never told her that I'm going to. We sit
close to each other but there are miles between our hands. 'And
now,' says my mother, 'just when she was going to enjoy life.'
'Yes,' I say, 'but she's not suffering anymore.' In spite of the late
hour, my mother makes coffee and we sit in my room drinking
it. 'Tomorrow,' says my mother, 'I'll have to go over to tell Aunt
Agnete. She's only visited her three times in all the time she's
been lying here.' When my mother begins to be outraged at
other people's behavior, she's temporarily saved from the deep-
est despair. She talks about how Aunt Agnete has never come
through when it mattered – even when they were children.
Then she always told on the other two and she always had to
be a little better than them. I let my mother talk and don't need
to say very much myself. I'm sorry that Aunt Rosalia is dead,
but not as much as I would have been as a child. That night I
sleep with an open window in spite of the ruckus from Bing
and Bang, and I look forward to having the rotten, suffocating
stench seep out of the apartment. Death is not a gentle falling asleep as I once believed. It's brutal, hideous, and foul
smelling. I wrap my arms around myself and rejoice in my youth
and my health. Otherwise my youth is nothing more than a
deficiency and a hindrance that I can't get rid of fast enough.

15

'It was all for your sake that we moved,' says my mother
bitterly. 'So that you could have a room to write in. But you
don't care. And now your father's unemployed again. We
can't do without what you pay at home.' My father sits up and
rubs his eyes. 'Yes,' he says fiercely, 'yes we can. Things are
pretty bad if you can't get by without your children. You sacrifice everything for them and just when you're going to have
a little pleasure from them, they disappear. It was the same
with Edvin.' 'It was a different matter with Edvin,' says my
mother. 'He's a boy.' She says it out of sheer contrariness, and
I breathe a little easier, because now it's become a fight
between the two of them. We're sitting in the dining room
eating dinner. It's become a habit that, because of my father's
varying work schedule, we eat a hot meal at noon, even
though it doesn't make any difference now. Because I'm
unemployed too. I was laid off from the office two weeks
before my birthday. But I've found a new job that I'm to start
the day after tomorrow, and I've also found a room. I'm
moving there tomorrow, and I've told my parents. While I
carry the plates out, they argue about it. 'She's heartless,' says

my mother crying, 'like my father. The night Rosalia died, she sat stiff as a board without shedding a single tear. It was really spooky, Ditlev.' 'No,' snaps my father, 'she's good enough at heart. You've just brought these children up all wrong.' 'And you,' yells my mother, 'haven't you brought them up? To be socialists and dry their snot in Stauning's beard. No, since Rosalia died, and now that Tove is moving out, I have nothing more to live for. You're always lying around snoring, whether you've got work or not. It's deadly boring to look at.' 'And you,' says my father furiously, 'you have nothing but your family and royalty in your head. As long as you can run off to the beauty salon every other minute, you don't care whether your husband is starving.' Now, fortunately, my mother is sobbing with rage and not with sorrow over my moving. 'Husband,' she howls, 'it's a hell of a husband I have. You don't even want to touch me anymore, but I'm not a hundred years old, and there are other men in the world!' Bang! She slams the door to the bedroom and throws herself onto the bed, continuing to sob so that you can probably hear it all over the building. I take the table-cloth off the table and fold it. Since we've moved to a better neighborhood, we don't use *Social-Demokraten* as a tablecloth anymore, and I don't have to look at Anton Hansen's gloomy drawings from Nazi Germany. My father rubs his hand hard over his face, as if he wants to move all of his features around, and says tiredly, 'Mother's in a difficult age. Her nerves aren't good. You ought to consider that.' 'Yes,' I say uncomfortably, 'but I want to live my own life, Father. I just want to be myself.' 'That's what you have your own room for, you know,' he says. 'There you can be yourself and write all the poems you want.' I despise it when they mention my poems – I don't know why. 'It's not just that,' I say on my way behind the

curtain. 'I want to have a place where I can invite my friends.'
'Well, yes,' he says, rubbing his face again, 'and Mother won't
allow that. But at any rate, you take good care of yourself.'
'Yes,' I promise, slipping at last into my own room. There I
pack up my few possessions, but I have to wait to empty the
dresser drawer in the bedroom until my mother has gone
into the dining room again. I've rented a room in Østerbro
because I don't think moving would be complete if I stayed in
Vesterbro. I don't like my landlady, but I took the room
anyway because it cost only forty kroner a month. I'm paying
off my winter coat and my dentist bill, but I'll have enough
money to get by, because at the Currency Exchange I'll get a
hundred kroner a month. My landlady is big and heavy. She
has wild, bleached hair and a dramatic demeanor, as if something catastrophic were about to happen any minute. In the
living room there hangs a big picture of Hitler. 'Look,' she
said when I rented the room, 'isn't he handsome? Someday
he'll rule the whole world.' She's a member of the Danish
Nazi Party and asked me whether I wanted to be a member
too, because they wanted to include the Danish youth. I said
no, I didn't have any sense for politics. And it's none of my
business what she's like. The main thing is that the room is
cheap. I move out there the next day. I ride over in the streetcar with my suitcase and my alarm clock, which won't fit into
the suitcase. It starts to ring between two stops and I smile
foolishly as I turn it off. It's a very temperamental alarm clock
that only I can operate. It's crabby and asthmatic like an old
man, and when it gets too sluggish and creaky, I throw it
onto the floor. Then it starts ticking, all gentle and friendly
again. The landlady greets me in the same loose-fitting
kimono that I saw her in the first time, and she looks just
as dramatic too. 'You're not engaged, are you?' she asks,

pressing her hand to her heart. 'No,' I say. 'Thank God,' she lets out her breath, relieved, as if she's avoided a dangerous situation. 'Men! I was married once, dear. He beat me black and blue whenever he'd been drinking, and I had to support him too. Things like that aren't allowed in Germany. Hitler won't stand for it. If people won't work, they get put in concentration camps. Does that alarm clock ring very loudly? I have such trouble sleeping and you can hear every sound in this house.' It rings so a whole county can hear it, but I swear that it's as good as soundless. At last she leaves me and I can calmly look over my new home. The room is quite small. There's a sofa with a flowered covering, an armchair in the same style, a table, and an old dresser with crooked, dangling handles on the drawers. There's a key in one of them, so I can really have something all to myself. In one corner there's a curtain with a rod behind it. It's supposed to serve as a wardrobe. There's also a chipped wash basin and pitcher. Furthermore, it's ice-cold here, like in Nina's room, and there's no stove. When I've put my clothes behind the curtain, I go out and buy a hundred sheets of typing paper. Then, with my last ten kroner, I rent a typewriter, which I place on the rickety table when I get back. I pull the armchair over to it, but when I sit down in it, the seat falls apart. All that I wanted for my forty kroner was a table and chair, but maybe you have to go up to a higher price category to get that. I go out and knock on the door to the living room where the landlady is sitting listening to the radio. 'Mrs Suhr,' I say, 'the chair broke. Could I borrow an ordinary chair?' She stares at me as if the news were a real misfortune. 'Broke?' she says. 'That was a perfectly good chair. It dates all the way back to my wedding.' She rushes in to inspect the damage. 'You'll have to give me five kroner for damages,' she says then, putting out her hand. I say that I don't have money until the first. Then she'll add it onto the rent, she says angrily. I follow her when she goes out again, begging her for an ordinary chair. 'It's highway robbery,' she huffs, massaging her heart again. 'It doesn't pay at all to rent out rooms. You'll probably wind up dragging men into my home, too.' She sends Hitler an imploring glance, as if he personally could throw out any men who might appear. Then she goes into the other room where there is a row of stiff, upright chairs along one wall. 'Here,' she says crossly, as she selects the most worn of them, 'take this one, then.' I thank her politely and carry it into my room. It's a good height for the table. Then I begin to type up my poems, and it's as if it makes them better. I'm filled with calm during this work, and the dream that this will someday be a book develops with stronger and clearer colors than before. Suddenly my landlady is standing in the doorway. 'That thing,' she says, pointing to the typewriter, 'makes a horrible racket. It sounds like machine guns.' 'I'm almost done,' I say. 'Otherwise I only type in the evening.' 'Well, all right.' She shakes her yellow-haired head. 'But not after eleven. You can hear every sound here. Say, wouldn't you like to hear Hitler's speech tonight? I listen to all of his speeches – they're wonderful. Manly, firm, resonant!' She gestures enthusiastically with her arm so you see her voluminous bosom. 'No,' I say alarmed, 'I . . . don't think I'll be home tonight.' But I *am* home because Nina has a visit from her forester, so I don't have anywhere to go. I sit and freeze even though I have my coat on, and I can't concentrate on writing because Hitler's speech roars through the wall as if he were standing right next to me. It's threatening and bellowing and it makes me very afraid. He's talking about Austria, and I button my coat at the neck and curl up my toes in my shoes.

Rhythmic shouts of 'Heil' constantly interrupt him, and there's nowhere in the room I can hide. When the speech is over, Mrs Suhr comes into my room with shining eyes and feverishly flushed cheeks. 'Did you hear him?' she shouts enraptured. 'Did you understand what he said? You don't need to understand it at all. It goes right through your skin like a steambath. I *drank* every word. Do you want a cup of coffee?' I say no thanks, although I haven't had a thing to eat or drink all day. I say no because I don't want to sit under Hitler's picture. It seems to me that then he'll notice me and find a means of crushing me. What I do would be considered 'decadent art' in Germany, and I remember what Mr Krogh said about the German intelligentsia. The next day I start my job at the Currency Exchange typing pool and Hitler invades Austria.

16

'Can you dance the carioca?' I look up from my shorthand and say no. I look at the secretary who I'm taking shorthand for; he's really handsome, but he doesn't take his work seriously. He sits lazily leaning back in the chair, now and then taking a gulp of the beer at his side. He yawns noisily without holding his hand in front of his mouth. 'Well,' he says tiredly, 'where were we?' We're sitting in a large room on the top floor. Here there are lots of desks with many secretaries. Whenever they need a typist, they phone down to our office and the supervisor sends one of us up. I like this work, but the secretaries bring me to despair. They would rather talk, and in the meantime the case lies in a blue folder on which it says 'urgent!' in red letters. There are applications for all kinds of things, and with each application there's a compelling letter implying that refusal of the enclosed will lead to suicide. Every single applicant writes about pressing, strictly personal reasons why *he* should be allowed to import his goods. I can dance the carioca just fine, but this is company time and I'm getting a high salary now, more than I've ever gotten before. 'Stop frowning,' says the secretary smiling, 'the wrinkles will end up being permanent.' I run down all the stairs and into the office to type up the letter. It's a rejection, and I try to make the tone of the letter kinder and less businesslike, just like I changed the letters to the brothers, but it isn't allowed here. I have to type it all over again and am requested to hold myself to the shorthand. There are about twenty of us young girls in the office, which looks like a schoolroom. There's a girl at every desk, and the desks are in three long rows. Farthest forward sits the supervisor, facing us like a teacher, and when the noise gets too intense, she hushes us sternly. All the other girls are very chic, with tight dresses, high heels, and a lot of makeup on their faces. One day one of them decides to make up my lips, my cheeks, and my eyes, and they all think I look much better that way. They say that I should wear makeup every day, and I start to borrow Nina's cosmetics when we go out in the evening. After I've typed up all of my poems, I can't stand sitting in my room with my teeth chattering from the cold. So I continue my nightlife with Nina, and even though it's rather monotonous, the days and nights fly by during this time, like a drumroll just before something's about to happen onstage. The terrible years at I. P. Jensen have passed; I'm eighteen; I've broken away from my family. One evening in the Heidelberg, I dance with a tall, blond young man who isn't like any of the usual young men and doesn't talk like them, either. He asks if he can treat me to a sandwich. I say that I'm with my girlfriend. He says that doesn't matter – then all three of us can have a sandwich. Nina looks at him approvingly and a little astonished when he introduces himself. His name is Albert and he's better dressed than the others. Maybe he's even a university student. We have sandwiches and beer, and I fumble with my knife and fork and watch to see how the others use the utensils. At home we cut up the food with the knife and then eat it with the fork. Albert asks me where I live and what I do. He asks me how much I earn and whether I can live on that. It's nothing special, but the other young men have never talked about anything but themselves. I have a tremendous desire to tell Albert everything about myself and my life. 'Maybe,' I say, 'I'll soon be able to earn more. I write poems, you see.' I don't like to say it, and especially not here, where there's so much noise, laughter, and music. But I don't feel that I can wait any longer and I don't know whether I'll ever see Albert again. 'Oh,' he says surprised, 'I didn't expect that. Are they good?' He smiles at me from the side, as if he's privately amused at me. That annoys me and I can feel that I'm blushing. 'Yes,' I say, 'some of them are.' 'Can you remember one of them by heart?' he says, munching. 'Yes, I can,' I say, 'but I don't want to say it here.' 'Then write it down,' he says calmly, pushing a napkin over to me. He takes a pencil out of his pocket and hands it to me. Which verse should I write? Which is the best of all? I feel that it's enormously important what I write, and after chewing on the pencil for a while, I write:

> I never heard your little voice.
> Your pale lips never smiled at me.
> And the kick of your tiny feet
> is something I will never see.

He looks thoughtfully at the verse for a long time and asks me what the poem is about. 'A child,' I say, 'stillborn.' He asks whether I've ever had a stillborn child, and I say no. 'I'll be damned,' he says then, regarding me with great curiosity. Nina is dancing with a young man and she winks at me encouragingly as they dance past the table. She thinks that I should make something of the situation, and I will too, in my own way. Albert follows my glance. 'Your girlfriend,' he says, 'is very pretty.' 'Yes,' I say, thinking that he wishes it were her he had chosen and not me. But I don't care about that side of the matter now. 'Do you know,' I say stubbornly, 'where you can send a poem like this to be published?' 'Oh, sure,' he says, as if I'd asked about something perfectly ordinary. 'Do you know a journal called *Wild Wheat*?' I don't, and he tells me that it's where young, unknown people can get their poems and drawings published. It's edited by a man named Viggo F. Møller, and he writes the name and address down on another napkin. 'I was out to see him recently,' he says so casually that it's clear that he's proud of it. 'He's very nice and he has a great understanding of young art.' I ask cautiously if he writes himself, and he says just as casually that in his spare time he has committed some verses to paper and a number of them have already been published in *Wild Wheat*. The news makes me totally speechless. I'm sitting next to a poet. It was more than I've ever dreamed of. I'm still silent when Nina returns. She lifts her fine eyebrows and thinks that Albert and I haven't gotten any further. 'In Heidelberg I lost my heart to the magic of a pair of eyes . . .' Everyone stands up and sings, as they swing the full beer steins back and forth. Albert has stood up too, and all of a sudden his posture expresses a certain impatience. I follow the direction of his glance and see, on the other side of the dance floor, a slight young girl, who's sitting alone and is very serious. When the music starts, Albert pays the bill, bows a little awkwardly to both of us, and asks the serious girl to dance. 'It was your own fault,' says Nina annoyed. 'He was really cute.' But actually I don't care. I've gotten hold of a corner of the world that I long for and I don't intend to let that corner go. I put the napkin in my purse and smile mysteriously at my girlfriend. 'I'm going home to type,' I say. 'If only the witch doesn't wake up.' 'You've gone from the frying pan into the fire,' Nina says. 'She's not a bit better than your mother.' I work my way to the cloakroom and get hold of my coat. I walk the whole way home even though it's bitter frost, and I feel very happy. A name and an address – how many years it can take to get that far. And maybe that's not even enough. Maybe this man won't want my poems. Maybe he'll die before they reach him. Maybe he's already dead. I should have asked Albert how old Viggo F. Møller is. I turn the name over and over and wonder what the 'F' stands for. Frants? Frederik? Finn? What if my letter never arrives because the postal service loses it? What if Albert has given me a totally wrong name and was putting one over on me? Some people think that kind of thing is so funny. Yet – deep inside I believe that this will work out. It's two in the morning when I tiptoe into my room. I fold the sofa blanket over several times and put it under the typewriter to dull the sound of it, and then I choose three poems that I send with a short, formal letter, so that the man won't think it's very important to me. 'Editor Viggo F. Møller,' I write, 'I am enclosing three poems in the hope that you will publish them in your journal, *Wild Wheat*. Respectfully and sincerely yours, T. D.' I run out to the nearest mailbox with the letter and look to see when it will be picked up. I want to figure out when the editor will get it and when he'll be able to answer it. Then I go home to bed, after first setting the alarm clock. I put all of my clothes on top of the comforter, but I still lie shaking from the cold for a long time before I fall asleep.

17

Every evening I rush home from the office and ask Mrs Suhr if there's a letter for me. There isn't, and Mrs Suhr is very curious. She asks if someone in my family is sick. She asks if I'm waiting for money in the mail, and reminds me of the five kroner that I owe her for the ruined chair. Once in a while she also asks me if I'm hungry, but I never am, even though I seldom eat dinner. Sometimes I eat at *Berlingske Tidende*'s canteen with Nina. It's cheap, but it's only for employees. My landlady also says that I'm getting thinner and thinner and if I were her daughter she'd fatten me up all right. When I notice the smell from the dinner that she's cooking, I get hungry after all, but then, of course, it's too late. Usually I drink a cup of coffee at Østerport station before going home, and I eat a piece of pastry with it. But that's a luxury that I really can't afford because I'm on a very strict budget. So are all of the girls in the office, even though most of them live at home. Toward the end of the month, they all borrow from each other, and they'd borrow from me too if I had anything to lend them. They're not hurt if you refuse. Their poverty isn't oppressive or sad because they all have something to look forward to; they all dream of a better life. I do too. Poverty is temporary and bearable. It's not any real problem. Nina has her mother to borrow from and she has The Shrub. Nina's mother is a fat and friendly woman who doesn't take anything too much to heart. She makes a living cleaning for people and she lives with a man who is the father of Nina's twelve- or thirteen-year-old half brother. You can tell immediately that Nina didn't grow up in that home but is only visiting. She's also only visiting in Copenhagen, and it's incomprehensible to me that she really wants to live in the country. While I'm waiting for the letter, I don't go out in the evening, but sit freezing in my room, listening for sounds from the hallway. I know that express letters can be delivered outside of the normal delivery times. There's no reason whatsoever why I should receive an express letter, but I listen for the doorbell just the same. One evening there's a political meeting at Mrs Suhr's, and a bunch of boot-clad men swarm into the living room where there is soon a terrible uproar. In the living room they click their heels together and shout 'Heil!' at the picture of Hitler. There are also a number of women present. Their voices are shrill like Mrs Suhr's, and as usual I hope that none of them will catch sight of me. They sing the Horst Wessel song and stamp on the floor so that the wall shakes from it. Mrs Suhr comes into my room, her cheeks red and her hair sticking out in all directions. She's still wearing her kimono and looks as if she's come running out of a burning house. 'Oh,' she gasps, 'won't you drink a toast to the Führer with us? Come in and say hello to all of these splendid fellows. Join us in fighting for our great cause.' 'No,' I say terrified, 'I have something I have to finish. Overtime work from the office.' I set myself to tapping at the typewriter so that they'll think I'm working, while I think with sorrow and uneasiness about the darkness that is about to descend over the whole world. But I don't forget to keep an ear tuned toward the hallway. Express letter, telegram – you never know . . . Several days later Mrs Suhr is standing in the hallway with a letter in her hand when I let myself in. 'Well,' she says with sensation-hungry eyes, 'here's that letter you've been waiting for.' I grab it out of her hand and want to go into my room but she blocks the way. 'Open it now,' she says breathlessly, 'I'm just as excited as you are.' 'No,' I say with a pounding heart, 'it's strictly private, confidential. It's a secret message, I must tell you.' 'Oh God!' She puts her hand to her heart and whispers, 'Something political?' 'Yes,' I say desperately, 'something political. Let me get by.' She looks at me as if I were a modern-day Mata Hari and finally backs away, deeply impressed. At last I'm alone with my letter. It's much too thick, and I grow weak in the knees with fear that the editor is sending it all back. I sit down by the window and look down at the little courtyard. The dusk wraps itself around the trash cans and the lights are being turned on in the building opposite. I open the envelope with an effort, take the letter out, and read, 'Dear Tove Ditlevsen: Two of your poems are, to put it mildly, not good, but the third, "To My Dead Child", I can use. Sincerely, Viggo F. Møller.' I immediately tear up the two poems that, to put it mildly, are not good, and then read the letter once again. He wants to publish my poem in his journal. He is the person that I've waited for all my life. I have a copy of *Wild Wheat* that I bought with money I borrowed from Nina. In it there's a poem by a woman – Hulda Lütken – and I've read it many times because I can't forget that my father once said that a girl can't be a poet. Even though I didn't believe him, his words made a deep impression on me. I have to share my joy with someone.

I don't feel like talking about it at home, and Nina wouldn't understand what it means to me. The only one who might is Edvin. He was the first to say that my poems were good, after he made fun of them. But that doesn't matter; we were only children then. I take the streetcar out to Sydhavnen. Grete opens the door and smiles, surprised at seeing me. 'Come in,' she says hospitably, and then runs in and sits down on Edvin's lap, which apparently is her main occupation as a newlywed. I think he looks completely defenseless in the deep armchair. 'Hi,' he says happily, 'how are you?' He has to move Grete's head in order to look at me. 'How are Mummy and Daddy?' asks Grete between two kisses. My mother can't stand this affectionate form of address, but Grete is completely insensitive to the coldness my mother exudes. I don't care much for Grete either, because I had always imagined that Edvin would have a beautiful, proud, and intelligent wife and not a little, smiling housewife of the Rubenesque type. But that doesn't really matter because my feelings aren't nearly as strong or as passionate as my mother's. I tell Edvin what has happened and show him the letter. He asks Grete to make coffee while he reads it. 'Wow,' he says impressed, 'you should get paid for this. He doesn't write a damn word about that. Be careful he doesn't cheat you.' I haven't thought about that at all, not for a moment. 'He earns money selling the journal, you know,' explains Edvin, 'so he shouldn't have unpaid contributors.' 'No,' I say. Not even Edvin understands what a miracle has occurred – no one understands it. 'Now listen here,' he says. 'You call him up and ask him what you're going to get for it.' 'Yes,' I say because I would like to call him up. I would like to hear his voice, and this is an excellent excuse. Grete sets the table and chatters on about nothing, and Edvin tells her about the letter. 'Oh,' she says happily, 'then I'm related to a poet. I'll write that to my parents. Would you like a couple of slices of bread?' 'Yes, thank you,' I say and ask how Edvin's cough is. The doctor said that he'll cough as long as he is spraying cellulose lacquer. He'll cough until he finds some other occupation. The doctor also says that it sounds worse than it is. He won't die from it, not even get really sick. His lungs are just black and irritated. While we drink coffee, I look at my brother. He doesn't seem happy, and maybe marriage isn't what he had expected. Maybe he had imagined a wife that he could talk to about something other than love and the evening meal. Maybe he had imagined that they could do something else in the evening other than sit on each other's lap and declare how much they love each other. I think, at any rate, that it must be just terribly boring. 'Don't you need a new dress soon?' says Grete. 'I've never seen you in anything except that cossack dress. You should get a permanent,' she says, 'like mine.' Grete's hair sits on top of her head in lots of little curls, and she wears big hoop earrings that clink when she shakes her head. 'Isn't it strange to have such a handsome brother?' she says. 'I think it must be very strange for you.' Edvin gets tired of her conversation and quickly sits down in the armchair again. After the cups are carried out, Grete settles herself on his lap once more and twists his black curls in her fingers. I think my brother has married her in order to escape sitting in his rented room with the stern landlady, because what other way out did he have? I don't intend to live at Mrs Suhr's for the rest of my life either. Being young is itself temporary, fragile, and ephemeral. You have to get through it – it has no other meaning. Edvin asks me whether I've told them the news at home, and I say that I want to wait until the poem appears in the journal. Then I'll show it to them, not before. Edvin reads the poem and is deeply impressed. 'But you're still full of lies,' he says with wonder in his voice. 'You've never had any dead child.' He says that Thorvald has gotten engaged to a very ugly girl, and it annoys me a little. I could have had him but I didn't want him. Still, I liked it that he wasn't attached to anyone else. Before I leave, I borrow ten øre from my brother to make a call. I have to let myself out because Grete is in the middle of a long whispering in Edvin's ear. In the telephone booth on Enghavevej, I look up Viggo F. Møller's number and ask for it with my heart in my throat from excitement. 'Hello,' I say, 'you are speaking with Tove Ditlevsen.' He repeats my name inquiringly and then he remembers it. 'Your poem will come out in a month,' he says. 'It's excellent.' 'Will I get any money for it?' I ask, very embarrassed. But he doesn't get angry. He just explains to me that no one gets an honorarium because the journal runs on a deficit, which he pays for out of his own pocket. I hurry to assure him that it doesn't matter, it was just something my brother said. Then he asks me how old I am. 'Eighteen,' I say. 'Good God – not more?' he says with a little laugh. Then he asks me whether I would like to meet him and I say that I would. He'll meet me the day after tomorrow, six o'clock, in the Glyptotek café, so we can eat dinner together. I thank him, overwhelmed, and then he says goodbye. I'm going to meet him. I'm going to talk to him. He undoubtedly wants to do something for me. Mr Krogh said that people always wanted to use each other for something, and that there was nothing wrong with that. It's quite clear what I want to use the editor for, but what does he want to use me for? Next evening I go home anyway and tell everything. My mother is home alone. She's very happy to see me, and I have a guilty conscience because I come over so seldom. My mother has grown very lonely since Aunt Rosalia's death.

The building is just 'fine' enough that you don't simply go running over to visit other people, and my mother doesn't have a single girlfriend she can talk to and laugh with. She only has us, and we deserted her as soon as she and the law would permit it. We drink coffee together and I can see that her imagination is hard at work. 'You know what,' she says, 'that editor – he probably wants to marry you.' I laugh and say that she never thinks of anything except getting me married. I laugh, but when I get home and into bed, I think about whether he's married or not. If he's single, I have nothing against marrying him. Entirely sight unseen.

18

He has on a green suit and green tie. He has thick, curly gray hair and a gray mustache, the ends of which he often twists between his fingers. He has an old-fashioned wing collar, and his double chin hangs over it a bit. His eyes are bright blue like little babies' eyes, and his complexion is pink and white and transparent like a child's. He makes wide, sweeping movements with his small, fine hands that have dimples at the knuckles. He is warm and friendly, and I quickly forget my shyness in his company. He doesn't resemble Mr Krogh in appearance and yet he reminds me of him a little. He studies the menu for a long time before he chooses what to have, and without knowing what it is, I ask for the same. He says that he's very fond of food, and that you can probably tell by looking at him. I say politely no. I admit that I never notice what I'm eating and he says, laughingly, that you can certainly tell by looking at me. I'm much too thin, he says. We drink red wine with our meal and I make a face because it's sour. He says that's because I'm so young. When I get older, I'll learn to appreciate good wine. He asks me to tell him a little about myself, about how I found my way to him. I'm nervous and light-hearted and want to tell everything at once. I also mention Albert, and he shrugs his shoulders as if he's no one in particular. 'You never can tell with young people,' he says, twisting his mustache. 'You believe in some of them, and then they don't amount to anything. Others you don't believe in, and it turns out that they're good after all.' I ask him whether he thinks I'm any good, and he says that you can't tell. He says that those who don't amount to much are those young men who come with a poem and say, 'I wrote this in ten minutes.' If they say that, he knows that they're not any good. 'And what then?' I ask. 'Then I advise them to be streetcar conductors or something else sensible,' he says, wiping his mouth with his napkin. I'm glad that I didn't write anything about how many minutes it took me to write 'To My Dead Child'. I don't even know myself. I think the editor is a magnificent man and I think he's handsome. Maybe others don't think he's handsome, and Nina would think that he's too old and fat, but I don't care. He gives me the menu so that I can order dessert, and I ask for ice cream because everything else looks much too complicated. The editor wants fruit with whipped cream. 'I have a sweet tooth,' he says, 'because I don't smoke.' The waiter treats him very respectfully and calls him 'the Editor' the whole time. He calls me 'the young lady'. 'May I pour for the young lady?' I bravely drink the sour wine and grow warm and relaxed from it. It's getting to be dusk outside and the wind is blowing softly in the trees on the boulevard. They're already in blossom, and soon Tivoli will open. Viggo F. Møller says that he loves spring and summer in the city. The trees and the flowers bloom, and the young girls blossom too, like beautiful flowers out of the cobblestones. Mr Krogh said something similar, and he wasn't married. That's probably something that married men

have no sense for at all. Finally I have the courage to ask him
if he's married, and he says no with a little laugh. 'No one,' he
says gesturing with his hand apologetically, 'has ever wanted
to have me.' 'I was formally engaged once,' I say, 'but then he
broke it off.' 'And now?' he asks. 'Aren't you engaged now?'
'No,' I say, 'I'm waiting for the right one to come along.' I try
to look him deep in the eyes, but he doesn't see the meaning
behind it. It's just that I've gotten used to the fact that everything is urgent, and I almost expect that he'll propose to me
right then and there. You never know where a person will be
tomorrow. He could get a letter from another young girl who
writes poems – Hulda Lütken, for example – invite her out,
and forget me completely. He must be the kind of man who
can have whomever he chooses. With growing jealousy I ask
how Hulda Lütken is, and he laughs loudly at the thought
of her. 'She wouldn't like you,' he says. 'She's insanely jeal-
ous of other women poets, especially if they're younger than
her. She's temperamental enough for ten. Once in a while
she calls me and says, "Møller, am I a genius?" "Yes, yes," I
say, "yes, you are, Hulda." Then she's satisfied for a while.'
Then he asks me if I'd like to come to a *Wild Wheat* party
next month. It's a party where the 'Top Wheat' and the 'Top
Rusk' are chosen. Those are the poet and the illustrator who,
during the year, have had the most contributions in the journal. I ask what I should wear, and he says a long dress. When
he hears that I don't have one, he says that I can borrow one
from a girlfriend. That makes me think of Nina, who got herself a long, backless dress for the dance at Stjernekroen. I say
that I would love to go to that party. We have coffee in very
thin cups and the editor looks at his watch, as if it's time to
go. I would have liked to sit there for a lot longer. Outside, my
daily life is waiting for me with its urgent matters at the office,

the evenings at the taverns, the young men who accompany me home, and my cold room with the Nazi landlady. My only consolation in this existence is a handful of poems, of which there are still not enough for a collection. And I don't know, either, how to go about publishing a poetry collection. When the bill is paid, Mr Møller suddenly places his hand over mine on the colorful tablecloth. 'You have beautiful hands,' he says, 'long and slender.' He pats my hand a couple of times, as if he knows very well that I'm sorry to leave and wants to assure me that he won't disappear from my life right away. I notice that I'm about to cry, and don't know why. I feel like putting my arms around his neck, as if I'm very tired after a long, long trip and now have finally found home. It's a crazy feeling and I blink my eyes a little to hide that they've grown moist. Outside we stand together for a while and look at the traffic. He's shorter than me, and that surprises me because you couldn't tell when he was sitting down. 'Well,' he says, 'I guess we're going different ways. Stop by some day. You know the address.' He swings his green, wide-brimmed hat in an elegant arc, puts it on his head, and walks quickly down the boulevard. I stand there and watch him for as long as my eyes can follow him. I think that I'm always having to say goodbye to men – staring at their backs and hearing their steps disappear in the darkness. And they seldom turn around to wave at me.

19

I've been moved over to the State Grain Office on the other side of the street, and I like it much better. There are just the two of us women in the office. I take care of the switchboard and I write letters for the office manager, Mr Hjelm. He's a tall, gaunt man with a long, grim face that is never softened by anything resembling a smile. Whenever there's a pause in the dictation, he stares at me as if he suspects that I have something other than grain in my head. The other girl is named Kate. She's quick to laugh and childish and we have a lot of fun together when we're alone. I'm waiting for my poem to be published in the journal, because then I'll visit Viggo F. Møller – not before. I'm going to have summer vacation soon, and that's always been a problem for me. Nina wants us to join the Danish Youth Hostel group and go hiking in the country and stay at youth hostels. But I don't like people in groups and I'm not interested in it. But if my poem comes out soon, maybe I can stay with the editor during my vacation. While I wait, I still look at the little children and the lovers who are driven out of the buildings by the heat. I look at the dogs too, the dogs and their masters.

Some of the dogs have a short leash that's jerked impatiently every time they stop. Others have a long leash and their masters wait patiently whenever an exciting smell detains the dog. That's the kind of master I want. That's the kind of life I could thrive in. There are also the masterless dogs that run around confused between people's legs, apparently without enjoying their freedom. I'm like that kind of masterless dog – scruffy, confused, and alone. I go out in the evening less often than before, and Nina says I'm getting to be downright boring. I stay in my room now that the cold doesn't chase me out anymore. I read my poems over and over again, and sometimes I write a new one. The two that were, to put it mildly, not good, I've long ago removed from my collection. I think they were hideous, but if the editor had written that they were good, I would have believed him. Sometimes I go home for a visit. My father is unemployed again and there's a cool atmosphere between him and my mother. Usually he's lying on the sofa, sleeping or dozing, and my mother sits knitting with a disapproving look on her face. She thinks it's about time I visit the editor because she's more and more convinced that he wants to marry me. 'Fat people,' she says, 'are happy and good-natured. It's the lean ones that are grumpy.' She asks how old he is, and I say that he's about fifty. That too she thinks is fine because then he's sown his wild oats and will make a faithful husband. She says that soon I can probably quit my job and be provided for. I say nothing because all of this has to wait. 'We'll hold the wedding,' says my mother, and I think about what my editor will say about his mother-in-law. He's older than she is, I'm pretty sure; but that doesn't bother my mother. I always leave soon because now my mother is demanding something of me. My father says that there's no rush and that it's up to me whom I want to marry. 'You've never cared much about it,' says my mother, 'but now you can see what's happened to Edvin. That's what you get for your indifference.' Then the battle has turned away from me and I have no qualms about leaving them. One day when I come home from my parents', I find a written eviction notice from Mrs Suhr. 'Since it has become known to me,' she writes, to my astonishment, 'that you have partici-pated in conspiratorial activities, I no longer wish to live under the same roof with you.' I remember the political letter that I received and my unwillingness to take part in her Nazi meetings. Then I find another room on Amager, not far from the editor's residence, and ride out there with my suitcase and my alarm clock in my hand. It's with a family that has grown children. A daughter has gotten married and it's her room that I move into. It's nicer and bigger than the other one and only ten kroner more. And on top of that, there's a stove. I immediately call Viggo F. Møller to tell him my new address, and he says it's good that I called because the journal has come out and he was just about to send it to me. He says it as if it were quite an everyday thing, as if I'd had dozens of poems published and this was just one of them. He says it in a friendly, ordinary tone, as if journals and books with my works were flooding the world so that it didn't matter so much whether such a trivial thing as a single poem got lost. But he is, of course, used to being around people like Hulda Lütken, people he's on a first-name basis with. Every time I think of her, I feel a stab of jealousy in my heart. I wonder whether Viggo F. Møller will ever tell peculiar things about me to other people? Will he say, 'Tove called recently, by the way, and said such and such. Ha, ha.' And twist his mustache and smile. The next day two copies of *Wild Wheat* arrive in the mail and my poem is in both of them. I read it many times and get an apprehensive feeling in my stomach. It looks completely different in print than typewritten or in longhand. I can't correct it anymore and it's no longer mine alone. It's in many hundreds or thousands of copies of the journal, and strange people will read it and may think that it's good. It's spread out over the whole country, and people I meet on the street may have read it. They may be walking about with a copy of the journal in their inside pocket or purse. If I ride in the streetcar, there may be a man sitting across from me reading it. It's completely overwhelming and there's not a person I can share this wonderful experience with. I rush home to show it to my father and mother. 'I think it's good,' says my mother, 'but you should have a pen name. The one you have isn't good. You should take my maiden name. Tove Mundus – that sounds much better.' 'Her name is good enough,' says my father, 'but the poem is much too modern. It doesn't rhyme in the right way. You could learn a lot from Johannes Jørgensen.' I'm not offended by my father's criticism because he has always wanted to protect us from disappointments. According to his experience, you should never expect anything from life, then you'll avoid disappointments. Still, he asks to be allowed to keep the journal, and he holds it in the same careful way as he does his books. On the way home, I go into a bookstore and ask for the latest edition of *Wild Wheat*. They don't have it but they can order one. 'We don't sell any of them as single copies,' the man explains to me, 'it's mostly by subscription.' 'That's too bad,' I say, 'you see, I've heard there's an excellent poem in it.' He takes down my name so I can get it in a couple of days. 'It's a very little journal, you know,' he explains talkatively. 'I think there are only five hundred copies printed. Strange that it can make a go of it.' Insulted, I go out of the store again. But I'm not the same as before. My name is in print. I'm not anonymous any longer. And soon I'll visit my editor, even though he didn't repeat his invitation on the phone. He has, of course, many other things to occupy him besides talking to young poets. A week after the journal came out, I'm called into Mr Hjelm's office. His long face is, if possible, even crabbier than usual and on the desk in front of him is *Wild Wheat* open to the page where my poem is. The thought flashes through my mind that he's going to praise me for it. 'I bought this journal,' he says, 'because I thought that it had something to do with grain. And then I see' – he strikes my poem with a ruler – 'that you apparently have other interests than the State Grain Office. I'm sorry, but unfortunately we can't use you here any longer.' He looks at me with his fish eyes and I don't know what to say. I feel bad because I was happy here, but there's also something comical about it that will make Kate and Nina laugh when I tell them. 'Yes,' I say, 'there's nothing to be done about it.' I edge my way out of the office and go in and tell Kate about being fired. She laughs that Mr Hjelm thought *Wild Wheat* was an agricultural journal, and I laugh too, but I'm still a girl who has lost her job and will now have the trouble of finding a new one. Kate says that I should report to the union and have them find a new position for me, and I think that's a good idea. The same evening I call Viggo F. Møller and he says that he would be happy to see me the following evening. Then it doesn't matter so much that I've been thrown out of the grain office. Maybe the editor can find a solution that is better than Kate's. I have so many expenses now that I can't allow myself to be unemployed.

20

'Wouldn't you like,' says Viggo F. Møller, 'to have a collection of poems published?' He says this as if it were nothing special. He says this as if it were quite common for me to publish poetry collections; as if it weren't what I've wished for, most fervently of all, for as long as I can remember. And I say with a thin, ordinary voice that yes, I would rather like that. I've just never thought of it before. But now that he mentions it, it would be great fun. I hope he can't tell how joyfully and excitedly my heart is pounding. It's pounding as if I were in love, and I look closely at this man who has caused such joy in my soul. He's sitting on the other side of the table, which is covered with a bottle-green tablecloth. We're drinking tea from green cups. The curtains are green, the vases and the pots are green, and the editor is wearing a green suit like before. The bookshelves reach almost up to the ceiling and the wall is completely hidden by paintings and drawings. It all reminds me of Mr Krogh's living room, but Viggo F. Møller doesn't remind me much of Mr Krogh. He's much less secretive and I'm welcome to ask him about anything I want to know. The sun is about to go down and there's a soft twilight in the living room that sets an intimate mood. I help my new friend carry the cups out to the kitchen and he asks me if I'd like a glass of wine. I say yes, thank you, and he pours wine into green glasses, lifts his and says, '*Skål.*' Then I ask him how you go about getting a poetry collection published, and he says that you send it to a publisher. Then they take care of the rest, if they accept the poems. It's very simple. I'm to show him all of the poems that I have so he can see if there are enough and if they're good enough. I don't care for the wine, but I like the effect. I'm very taken with the editor's soft, round arm movements, with his silver-gray hair and his voice, which wraps itself soothingly and refreshingly around my soul. I'm already fond of him, but I don't know what his feelings are for me. He doesn't touch me and doesn't try to kiss me. Maybe he thinks that I'm too young for him. I ask him why he's not married and he says gravely that no one wanted him. It's sad, he says, but now he figures that it's too late. He has a smile in his eyes when he says this, and I frown because he doesn't take me seriously. I tell him about my life, about my parents, about Edvin, and about how I've just lost my job because of the poem in *Wild Wheat*. The latter amuses him greatly and he says that it will amuse his friends too, when he tells them about it. His friends are celebrities, and some of them have asked him who the poor young girl is who wrote so beautifully about her dead child. So it's not just my family who thinks everything you write is true. 'Oh,' he says, slapping his forehead, 'I almost forgot. Did you see Valdemar Koppel's review of the journal in *Politiken* recently? He writes very positively about your poem.' He takes out the clipping and shows it to me. It says: 'A single poem, "To My Dead Child", by Tove Ditlevsen is justification enough for the little journal's existence.' 'Oh,' I say overwhelmed, 'how happy that makes me. May I keep it?' He gives it to me and he pours more wine into the green glasses. Then he says, 'It makes a strong impression on a young person to see their name in print for the first time.' 'I'm so glad that I met you,' I say. 'It's as if nothing bad can happen when I'm with you. When I'm here, I don't believe there'll be a world war.' Viggo F. Møller grows suddenly serious. 'It looks very bleak otherwise,' he says. 'I can probably do something or other for you, my dear, but I can't prevent the world war.' It's the wine that makes me say such things. All the grownups withdraw from me whenever they start thinking about the world situation. In comparison, my poems and I are just specks of dust that the smallest puff of wind can blow away. 'No,' I say, 'but you're not going to suddenly die and this building isn't going to be torn down.' I tell him about Editor Brochmann and Mr Krogh. The former he knew, but not the latter. 'No,' he says seriously, 'in that sense you can rely on me. Why don't we use our first names?' We toast our friendship and he turns on the lights in the green-shaded lamps. 'Call me Viggo F.,' he says then. 'Everyone calls me Viggo F. or Møller – no one calls me Viggo except my family.' His parents, he says, are dead, but he has a brother and a sister whom he rarely sees. 'Families,' he says, 'never understand artists. Artists only have each other to rely on.' He asks me if I'd like to sit next to him on the sofa, and I sit down by him. I sit close to him so that our legs are touching each other, but it apparently doesn't make any impression on him. Maybe I'm not pretty enough; maybe I'm not old enough. He tells me that he's fifty-three years old, and I say politely that he doesn't look it. He doesn't either, aside from the fact that he's fat. His skin is pink and white and totally free of wrinkles. I think my father looks much older. But for that matter I don't care a bit about how old people are. Viggo F.'s father was a bank director and his brother is, too. He himself works for a fire insurance company, which he doesn't care for, but you've got to earn a living somehow. He has also written books, and I'm embarrassed that I haven't read them. I haven't even run across his name in the library. My ignorance irritates me and I tell my new friend that I was supposed to go to high school but I wasn't allowed to. We couldn't afford it. Gently he puts his arm around my waist and a hot stream races through me. Is this love? I'm so tired of my long search for this person that I feel like crying with relief, now that I've reached my goal. I'm so tired that I can't return his tender, cautious caresses, but just sit passively and let him stroke my hair and pat my cheeks. 'You're like a child,' he says kindly, 'a child who can't really manage the adult world.' 'I once knew someone,' I say, 'who said that all people want to use each other for something. I want to use you to get my poems published.' 'Yes,' he says, continuing to caress me, 'but I don't have as much influence as you think. If the publishers don't want your poems, I can't do anything. But we'll take a look at them. I can advise you and support you, at any rate.' When I go out to the bathroom, I see that Viggo F. has a shower, and it overwhelms me. I ask him if I can take a shower, and he says yes, laughing. Otherwise I go once in a while to the public baths on Lyrskovgade, but it costs money, of course, so it's never been very often. Now I stand delighted under the shower, twisting and turning, and thinking that if we really get married, I'll take a shower every single day. When I come out of the bathroom, Viggo F. says, 'You have nice legs. Lift up your dress so I can see them properly.' 'No,' I say, blushing, because I have a run in one stocking. 'No, they're only nice from the knees down.' It's gotten to be twelve o'clock and I have to go home to my wretched room. Viggo F. offers to pay for a cab home, but I say that I can certainly walk the short distance. And I add, 'I can't figure out what I'm supposed to give the cabbie as a tip, anyway.' 'Remember to call him "driver", not "cabbie". That sounds too colloquial.' The remark hurts me and I get furious at my whole upbringing, at my ignorance, my language, my complete lack of sophistication and culture, words I hardly understand. He kisses me on the mouth when he says goodbye, and I walk through the mild summer night and recall all of his words and movements. I am not alone anymore.

21

I've been with many celebrities. I've seen them, I've talked to them, I've sat next to them, I've danced with them. As soon as I stepped in the door, I was moving on a completely different plane than usual. I walked in a glaring light and cast the rays of the celebrities back like a mirror. I reflected their images, and they liked what they saw. Flattered, they smiled and gave me many compliments. They even praised my dress, although it is Nina's and it's too big for me. But it hid my shoes, which are old and worn and need to be replaced. The celebrities constantly gathered in clusters around Viggo F.'s green shape, which appeared and disappeared like duckweed on a windy pond. It swelled back and forth before my eyes, and I repeatedly sought it out because it was my protection and my security among all the celebrities. Viggo F. introduced me to them with pride, as if he had invented me. 'My youngest contributor,' he said to the press photographers, smilingly twisting his mustache. I was photographed with him and some of the celebrities, and the picture was in *Aftenbladet* the next day. It wasn't very good, but Viggo F. said that it was important to be friendly toward the press. And I was friendly.

I smiled the whole evening to all of the celebrities who wanted to meet me, and in the end my cheeks hurt. My feet also hurt from dancing, and when I finally left, the whole thing was as unreal as a dream. I couldn't remember who had become the 'Top Wheat' and the 'Top Rusk'. But a young man I danced with said that everyone was chosen eventually. I, too, would someday be the 'Top Wheat', it was just a matter of writing a lot for the journal, regardless of whether it was good. The young man also asked me if I wanted to go to the movies some evening, but I turned him down coldly. I had quite different plans for my future. I've gotten a job as a temporary through the union and now I'm earning ten kroner a day. I've never had so much money in my hands before. I've paid the dentist bill and I've bought a light gray suit with a long jacket because the brown one had gone out of style. I don't spend much time with Nina anymore, because now I'm totally uninterested in meeting a young man who might want to marry me. After Viggo F. looked at my poems and selected some of them, I sent them to Gyldendal Publishing Company and now I'm going around waiting for an answer. 'If they don't want them,' says Viggo F., 'you just send them to another one. There are plenty of publishers.' But I'm certain that they'll want them, since Viggo F. says they're good. He knows the director, who is a woman. Her name is Ingeborg Andersen and she dresses like a man. 'But she's not the one who will decide,' says Viggo F., 'it's the consultants.' They are Paul la Cour and Aase Hansen, and I don't know either of them. I don't know any of the celebrities because I almost never read newspapers and have only read authors long since dead. I've never realized before that I was so dumb and ignorant. Viggo F. says that he'll take care of getting me a little education, and he lends me *The French Revolution* by Carlyle. I find it very exciting, but I would rather start with the present day. One evening when I'm visiting Viggo F., the doorbell rings and I hear a low female voice out in the hallway. Viggo F. comes in with a sparkling, plump, dark little woman who shakes my hand as if she means to tear it off, and says, 'Hulda Lütken. Huh . . . so that's what you look like. You're becoming so celebrated it's almost unbearable.' Then she sits down and speaks the whole time to Viggo F., who finally asks me to leave, because there's something he wants to talk to Hulda about. Later he explains to me – what he has already hinted at – that Hulda Lütken can't stand other female poets. While I'm waiting to hear from Gyldendal, I sometimes go home to visit my parents. My father says that of course it would be fun if I had a poetry collection published, but that you can't make a living as a poet. 'She won't have to, either,' says my mother, eager to fight. 'That Viggo F. Møller – he can support her.' I tell them about the shower and, in her thoughts, my mother also stands under Viggo F.'s shower. I tell them about the wine in the green glasses and, in her thoughts, my mother drinks from them too. They have cut out the picture from *Aftenbladet* and put it in the frame of the sailor's wife. 'It's good,' says my mother. 'You can really see that you've had your teeth fixed.' She says with pride, 'The doctor says that I have high blood pressure. I also have hardening of the arteries and a bad liver.' She's gotten a new doctor because the old one was no good. Whatever you said was wrong with you, he said that he suffered from the same thing. The new doctor agrees with all of my mother's suspicions and she is devoted to him. Since Aunt Rosalia died and both Edvin and I have moved out, she's very absorbed with her health, even though she never gave it a thought before. She's going through the change of life, the doctor said, and the people around her must be considerate of her. That's what she told my father, who never dares lie down on the sofa anymore, which she always has nagged him about. He sits up and reads and sometimes he falls asleep with the book in his hand. I never stay home for very long because I get tired of listening to my mother's alarming symptoms from her inner organs. But I feel sorry for her because she never had very much in this world, and the little she had, she lost. One day when I come home from work, there is a big, yellow envelope lying on the table in my room. My knees grow weak with disappointment because I know what it contains. Then I open it. They have sent my book back with a few apologetic sentences, to the effect that they only publish five poetry collections a year, and they've already chosen them. I take the letter and go over to Viggo F. with it. 'Oh well,' he says, 'it was to be expected. We'll try Reitzel's Publishing Company. Don't let yourself be beaten by something like this. Trust in yourself, otherwise you'll never get anyone else to.' We send the poems to Reitzel's and a month later they're sent back. I think it's starting to get interesting because I know that the poems are good. Viggo F. says that almost every famous writer has been through the mill – yes, there's almost something wrong if it goes too smoothly. Finally the poems have almost made the entire rounds, and it's hard to keep up my courage. Then Viggo F. says that it's a question of money. The publishers make almost nothing on poems; that's why they're reluctant to publish them. But *Wild Wheat* has a fund of five hundred kroner meant for cases like mine. He'll give the money to a publisher to publish the poems. He'll talk to his friend, Rasmus Naver, about the matter. Mr Naver agrees to publish the poems at his company, and I am happy. He comes over to Viggo F.'s to talk to him about it. He's a kind, gray-haired gentleman with a Fyn accent, and I smile at him sweetly the whole time so that nothing about me will make him give up the idea. He says that Arne Ungermann would probably draw the cover without a fee, and he likes the title: *Pigesind*, or 'Girl-Soul'. I like it too. Finally it's worked out and I don't know how to show Viggo F. my gratitude. I kiss him and ruffle his curly hair, but he is so absent-minded lately. It's as if he does want to do something for me, but he has something more important on his mind at the moment. One evening he tells me about the concentration camps in Germany and says that all of Europe will soon be one concentration camp. He also shows me a journal in which he has written an article against Nazism and he says that it will be dangerous for him if the Germans ever come to Denmark. I think about my poetry collection that will come out in October and have a strange feeling that it will never appear if the world war breaks out. 'If they go into Poland,' says Viggo F., 'the English won't stand for it.' I say that they have put up with so much. I tell him about my time at Mrs Suhr's. I tell him that every time I heard Hitler speaking through the wall on Saturday, he invaded some innocent country on Sunday. Viggo F. says that he can't understand why I didn't move out before, and I think that he doesn't know what it is to be poor. But I don't say anything. Arne Ungermann comes over one evening and shows me the cover drawing. It depicts a naked young girl with bowed head, and it's very beautiful. The figure is chaste and devoid of all sensuality. He and Viggo F. talk about the world situation and are very serious. Now I'm almost always at Viggo F. Møller's, and my mother thinks that I might just as well move in with him. 'When,' she says impatiently, 'do you intend to marry him?'

22

Edvin has left his wife. Now he's living at home in my old room behind the cotton curtain, and my mother is happy, even though he's going to move as soon as he can find a room. My mother says that she can understand why he left Grete, because she only had clothes and nonsense in her head and no man can put up with that. But my brother won't allow anyone to put Grete down. He says that the mistake was his. He didn't love her, and that wasn't her fault. That's also why he has let her keep the apartment. She gets to keep the furniture too, and Edvin will continue to make the payments. I like coming home now that my brother is there. We talk about my poetry collection, and Edvin can't understand why you don't get paid for something like that. 'It's a piece of work,' he says, 'and it's despicable that it's not paid for.' We also talk about Edvin's cough and about all of my mother's new illnesses. We talk about my work at a lawyer's office in Shellhuset, where I get to observe many disagreements between people. And we talk a lot about Viggo F. Møller and the world that he has opened for me. I have to tell my family everything about his apartment – how the furniture is arranged, how many rooms there are, and what books are on the bookshelves. I tell my father that Viggo F. writes books himself, and he says that he thinks he's read one of them once, but that it was nothing special. My father also says, 'Isn't he too old for you?' My mother protests and says it's not age that matters, and it never has bothered her that my father is ten years older than she is. She says the most important thing is that he can support me, so I can quit working. They all talk as if he has already proposed to me, and when I say that I don't know if he will have me, they brush the question aside as a minor detail. 'Of course he will have you,' says my mother. 'Why else would he do so much for you?' I think about that and come to the same conclusion. The different thing about me is that I write poetry, but at the same time there's a lot that is ordinary about me. Like all other young girls, I want to get married and have children and a home of my own. There's something painful and fragile about being a young girl who makes her own living. You can't see any light ahead on that road. And I want so badly to own my own time instead of always having to sell it. My mother asks me what Viggo F. makes at the fire insurance company, and she thinks it's strange that I have no idea. 'He's just a white-collar worker,' says my father, full of contrariness, invoking an indignant stream of words from both my mother and Edvin. 'If I were a white-collar worker,' says Edvin angrily, 'I would never have gotten this damned cough.' 'At any rate there's no risk,' my mother seconds him, 'of him being unemployed at any minute and loafing around with a book while decent people go to work. Feel my neck,' she says to me suddenly. 'It's as if there's a knot right here. I'll have to show it to the doctor. We'll hire a cook for the wedding – he's of course used to the best. Soup, roast, and dessert – I remember well how it was at the places where I worked. Couldn't you invite him home some day?' I don't know why I don't do that. My family is mine. I know them and am used to them. I don't like having them displayed to someone from a higher social class. Viggo F. has even asked me if he could meet my parents. He says he would like to meet the people who have produced such an odd creature as me. But I think that can wait until we get married. My father and Edvin also talk about the imminent world war. Then my mother gets bored and I lose my good humor. Suddenly it's a fact. England has declared war on Germany, and I stand with thousands of other silent people and follow the reader-board headlines flashing on *Politiken*'s building. I stand next to my brother and my father and I don't know where Viggo F. is at this fateful hour. When we go home, I have a painful, sinking feeling in my stomach, as if I were very hungry. Will my poetry collection come out now? Will daily life continue at all? Will Viggo F. marry me when the whole world is burning? Will Hitler's evil shadow fall over Denmark? I don't go home with them but take a streetcar out to my friend's. There are a lot of celebrities at his house, and he doesn't seem to notice me. They're drinking wine from the green glasses and talking very seriously about the situation. Ungermann asks me what I think of his drawing, and I thank him for it. So the book will probably come out after all. I go home without really having talked to Viggo F., and at night I dream uneasily about the world war and *Pigesind*, as if there really were a fateful connection between them. But already the next day it's clear that daily life will go on as if nothing had happened. At the office the divorce cases, property line disputes, and other heated disagreements between people pile up. Excited people stand at the counter asking for the attorney, who is seldom there, and I have to listen to them present their special, terribly important case, and no one seems to remember that a world war broke out yesterday. My landlady tells me that pork has gone up fifty øre per kilo, and Nina comes over to confide in me that she's met a wonderful young man, and she's thinking of dropping The Shrub again. Nothing at all has changed, and when I go over to Viggo F.'s, he is again in a good mood, radiating calm and coziness in great, warm waves. 'In three weeks,' he says, 'your book will come out. Soon you'll have to read the proofs, but you shouldn't let it get you down. Reading the proofs, you never think it's good enough. It's like that for everyone.' Viggo F. isn't the least bit interested in ordinary people. He only likes artists and only spends time with artists. Everything about me that is quite ordinary, I try to hide from him. I hide from him that I like the new dress that I've bought. I hide the fact that I use lipstick and rouge and that I like to look at myself in the mirror and turn my neck around almost out of joint in order to see what I look like in profile. I hide everything that could make him have misgivings about marrying me. He's right about the proofs. When they arrive, I don't care for my poems at all anymore, and I find many words and expressions that could be better. But I don't correct very much because Viggo F. says that then the printing will be too expensive. In the days before the book comes out, I stay home in my room all the time that I'm not in the office. I want to be there when my book is delivered. One evening when I come home, there's a big package lying on my table, and I tear it open with shaking hands. My book! I take it in my hands and feel a solemn happiness, that isn't like anything I've ever felt before. Tove Ditlevsen. *Pigesind*. It can't be taken back anymore. It is irretrievable. The book will always exist, regardless of how my fate takes shape. I open one of the books and read some lines. They are strangely distant and foreign, now that I see them in print. I open another book because I can't really believe that it says the same thing in all of them. But it does. Maybe my book will be in the libraries. Maybe a child, who in all secrecy is fond of poetry, will someday find it there, read the poems, and feel something from them, something that the people around her don't understand. And that odd child doesn't know me at all. She won't think that I'm a living young girl who works, eats, and sleeps like other people. Because I myself never thought about that when I read books as a child. I seldom remembered the names of those who wrote them. My book will be in the libraries and maybe it will be in the windows of bookstores. Five hundred copies of it have been printed, and I've been given ten. Four hundred and ninety people will buy it and read it. Maybe their families will read it too, and maybe they'll lend it out like Mr Krogh lent out his books. I will wait to show the book to Viggo F. until tomorrow. Tonight I want to be alone with it, because there's no one who really understands what a miracle it is for me.